CARIBBEAN WRITERS SERIES

18

The Leopard

6.00

CARIBBEAN WRITERS SERIES

THE LEOPARD

V. S. Reid

Introduction by Mervyn Morris
University of the West Indies

HEINEMANN
LONDON · KINGSTON · PORT OF SPAIN

Heinemann Educational Books Ltd
22 Bedford Square, London WC1B 3HH
P.O. Box 1028, Kingston, Jamaica
27 Belmont Circular Road, Port of Spain, Trinidad
IBADAN   NAIROBI
EDINBURGH   MELBOURNE   AUCKLAND
SINGAPORE   HONG KONG   KUALA LUMPUR   NEW DELHI

British Library Cataloguing in Publication Data

Reid, Victor Stafford
  The Leopard. – (Caribbean writers series; 18).
  I. Title
  II. Series
  823'.9'1F   PR9265.9.R/

  ISBN 0-435-98660-0

Set, printed and bound in Great Britain by
Cox & Wyman Ltd, Reading

To Anne

Introduction

For many years white propaganda concerning the Mau Mau period in Kenya (about 1952 to about 1957) 'tended to present a one-sided and distorted view of reality – that of the *noble white man* who, fervently engaged in bringing civilization, Christianity, education and the "good life" to Kenya's backward natives, was suddenly forced to defend self and property, law and order, peace and morality, against the treacherous attack of *atavistic* savages gone mad with blood lust.'[1] More recently, in such books as *Mau Mau from Within* (1966) from which the quotation is taken, and *The Myth of 'Mau Mau': Nationalism in Kenya* (1966),[2] there has been scholarly concern to understand the human and historical reasons underlying Mau Mau, the revolt of a large section of the people of Kenya.

V. S. Reid is the author of *New Day* (1949) and other historical novels of Jamaican nationalism. Reid's *The Leopard* (first published in 1958) is a black Jamaican's imaginative rejection of anti-Mau Mau propaganda. In this novel the blacks are far from perfect, but they are fully human beings; they have a culture, history morality, religion; they experience a wide range of human emotion.

In the particular circumstances, however, hate and an impulse to revenge are driving forces:

It is a rich land: rich in humus and equally rich in hate, for all men

[1] Donald L. Barnett and Karari Njama, *Mau Mau from Within* (Monthly Review Press, New York & London, 1966), p. 17.
[2] Carl G. Rosberg, Jr., and John Nottingham, *The Myth of 'Mau Mau': Nationalism in Kenya* (Praeger, New York & London, 1966).

vii

crave it. Know, therefore, it is a land of feud: for the white challenger wants to conquer it, and the black man to keep it. (p. 8)

From very early the novel establishes, as a basic assumption, that the blacks are the true owners of the land in Kenya.

But the bwanas stole farms without a wink, farms a day's journey to cross. (p. 21)
Nebu ... had been a retainer in one of the stone houses on the Kenya slope built where his fathers had once herded their cattle (p. 9)

In *Facing Mount Kenya* (first published in 1938) Jomo Kenyatta describes the injustice in a bitter fable: an elephant, having been allowed to put his trunk inside the hut, gradually forces the original owner out into the rain, then has his occupancy legitimized by a hypocritical Commission of Inquiry: 'We consider that Mr Elephant has fulfilled his sacred duty of protecting your interests ... Mr Elephant shall continue his occupation of your hut, but we give you permission to look for a site where you can build another hut more suited to your needs, and we will see that you are well protected.' Then the process is repeated, with new beneficiaries former Commissioners, friends of Mr Elephant.[3]

Mau Mau was an intensification of the struggle of black Kenyans to recover their land and their freedom. The white man was the enemy, and, as in other situations of war, the enemy is dehumanized, conjured up as an appropriate object of hate.

Now it is a fact that Nebu was hurrying towards a murder, but it did not appear in that way to him at all. To him, he was stalking a dangerous man-animal. An animal you could never get upwind of, for he had no upwind nor downwind. He was a gun: he hid a mile away behind a tree and slew you. And you were able to hate him as you could never hate a lion, for a lion never ignored your customs, nor laughed at them. A lion was even willing to share his land with you provided you took the day and allowed him abroad at night. (pp. 17–18)

The young lieutenant at the mouth of the cave is not, in the eyes of

[3] Jomo Kenyatta, *Facing Mount Kenya* (Heinemann, London, 1979), pp. 50–1.

Nebu, human; he is a cowardly beast, a dangerous man-animal, a leopard to be killed. The castrating policeman so deftly tortured by the Kikuyu women (p. 10) and the policeman whipped to death with loving care (pp. 53–4) are seen as representatives of the evil enemy. In the exultant hatred engendered in total combat they are not seen as persons. 'Have nothing to do with the white man – except to make him beautiful,' Koko frequently raved, 'and he is only beautiful when he dies of Mau Mau!' (p. 18.)

The reader of *The Leopard* is not, however, invited into total identification with racial hate, even as revenge. That word 'raved', suggesting detachment from the attitudes of Koko, is one indication. The repulsive details of Gibson's death are another. (pp. 24–6.) The novelist is surely aware that only by a perversion of language can one describe this death as 'being made beautiful'; the language of Koko, cheer-leader of hate, is being undermined.

Although Nebu has been taught to hate white people in general, and to 'make them beautiful', particular white individuals present him with problems. Face to face with the white victim he has stalked for days, Nebu experiences a moment of fatal hesitation: he is torn between his duty to kill the white man and a morality which forbids him to kill this particular white man, a particular person he has wronged. Remembering Msabu Gibson, Nebu refuses to deem her less desirable than his sweet black bride: '*Is today's rain different from yesterday?*' he asks. (p. 96.) The msabu's importance in the novel is partly that she has acknowledged Nebu as a human being, accepting not only his potency but also his affection. In the description of their sexual encounter there is emphasis on her giving: 'using the rich language of her body to talk away his fears ... opening the blouse to offer and offer.' (p. 14.) Disconcertingly for her husband, she is unperturbed by Nebu's little signals of his devotion. Bwana recommends distrust: 'You've got to be careful of them. There's some trouble brewing in Nairobi. Some terrorist gang springing up.' (p. 16.) Even in dying Bwana Gibson keeps his distance from Nebu: he will not acknowledge their common humanity:

'Look – look at me, black swine,' he said softly. 'Dy-ing like a white man. Do you – see – me – begging?'

But neither would I, Nebu thought . . . Why cannot the white man understand?' (p. 25)

The Leopard constantly reminds us that black and white share a common condition. The loins are blind. (p. 96.) 'The worms know no colour.' (p. 49.) Equally, however, it presents two cultures of differing tendency. The blacks are represented as in harmony with nature, in close touch with the rhythms of the earth. 'The land was a book you learnt to read.' (p. 15.) The world the whites prefer is largely man-made. The white man is easily lost in the bush, the black man in the towns. (p. 13.) But each has been learning the other's skills; the English have become good bushmen since the Emergency, and the Africans are acquiring the white man's guns.

The rifle is one of the novel's central symbols. An instrument of destruction, it is the source of many disasters. Nebu sets off on the trail of the white man in the hope of getting a rifle. Bwana Gibson is killed for it, Nebu is wounded by it. Toto, also, is a victim of it: had he not withheld the bolt, he might have been made safe from the leopard. Since the rifle (which is phallic) has to be earned by murdering an enemy, it becomes for the guerrilla a symbol of manly achievement: 'the rebuff to his spirit by the elusive rifle was real as an aching cavity.' (p. 6.) It is valued like a woman: Nebu 'could go to bed with such a gun.' (p. 32.) It is authority: Koko, the guerrilla leader, had two. It is power. 'It had made gods of the white men.' (p. 16.) Acquiring a rifle Nebu feels changed: 'A godlike feeling.' (p. 32.) 'He was gifted with destruction.' (p. 32.) But, perhaps most importantly, the rifle is foreign to Nebu (p. 27); even when he comes to think it does not look alien in his hand, he cannot make it function. (p. 87.) Toto, half-European, knows more about the European weapon, but, with characteristic malice, uses his knowledge to frustrate the African. By the time Toto deems it necessary, in his own interest, to restore the rifle bolt, Nebu has learnt to distrust the alien instrument: ' "I know the spear. A great warrior is sensible. He does not ride a strange horse over a narrow footbridge." ' (p. 101.)

The novel seems to support a cautious acceptance of change. M'lodi has made the mistake of undervaluing the traditional weapons, which in particular circumstances might well be more efficient: with bow and arrow, for example, game could be silently hunted, as Nebu had suggested. Towards the end of the novel, Nebu reflects that he may owe his own death to inflexible respect for tradition, for 'the old customs': he believed it his duty to take Toto to Nairobi as a recompense for having wronged Gibson: 'He said sadly: "M'lodi, the unnatural, was right. I should have been strong and lost the bow, for the days of the bow have gone." ' (p. 106.) Yet it is one of the traditional weapons, and an old skill, which gives Nebu his final moment of triumph: ' "With evening sitting in my belly, even then I can throw" ', he boasted (p. 107.) With the enemy framed in the door of the cave, Nebu summoned the old skill and what remained of his strength: 'It was morning in his arms and shoulders.' (p. 108.) A new day, of black power, dawns.

Like the rifle, the leopard is important as its literal self and as a symbol whose significance shifts. We are very early told that the leopard 'avoids the strong and eats the wounded and the weak.' (p. 8.) More often than not, he is clearly identified with the whites: with Bwana Gibson, for example, 'the night the bwana had become an animal, shrieking and battering-in the flower face of the msabu as she lay spent and weak after the birth …' (p. 17.) The identification is reinforced when, at the end, the flower image is recalled: the msabu's son, struck down by the literal leopard, is, according to the army lieutenant: ' "Like a bloody muddy flower on a bloody broken stem." ' (p. 108) The identification is suggested even in jokes: when Toto, uncertain of his safety, points out that there are wild beasts on the road, Nebu sharply remarks: ' "In the towns too." ' (p. 69.) When, meaning the leopard, Toto inquires: ' "You think he will be back today?" ' Nebu asks: ' "Who? Your father?" ', meaning Bwana Gibson (p. 72.) In the final moments of the book the young army lieutenant is targeted as 'a lean-waisted, wide-shouldered, tawny bull leopard'. (p. 108.)

The leopard is not only cowardly and dangerous, he is associated with ultimate evil and with original sin. He has a 'demoniac' head, (p. 17) and just where there has been 'foliage green as Eden ... Nebu saw the ugly evil waiting for him, disfiguring the beautiful valley, horrifying to him as a mamba coiled in a Communion cup.' (p. 35.) The leopard has a narrow forehead that bears 'a curious resemblance to the serpent's'. (p. 35.)

Original sin cannot be reserved for the whites. 'Both sides were full of sinners.' (p. 22.) Because the novel's point of view is most often Nebu's, the finger is most often pointed at the whites. But the blacks too, and of course the mulato Toto, attack the wounded and the weak. In the first paragraph the guerrillas strike 'when the morning ebb had drained the vigilance from the beleaguered settlers'. (p. 3.) Nebu's stalking of the white man is very much like the leopard's stalking of Nebu: Nebu 'knew that the leopard would not attack while he thought his victim strong and ready'. (p. 105.) We recall how patiently Nebu waited for the rifle-bearing white man to be off guard. (p. 23.) The army lieutenant at the end is not, of course, attacked when he is ready. 'He dropped his arm and walked forward.' (p. 108.) It is then that Nebu attacks. The leopard is Brother Leopard as well as Bwana Leopard.

With Nebu weakened by a festering wound, Toto deliberately turns over a kettle of boiling water on him, and, once elevated to Nebu's shoulders, he is pleased to aggravate the wound by kicking him in it. In one of his many moments of treachery, Toto interrupts Nebu's healing soak in the sulphur pool by crying out 'The leopard! ... Nebu, the leopard.' (p. 77.) When Nebu goes after the crutch supposedly thrown at the leopard he has to deal with a mamba, a serpent and the reader recalls the passage earlier associating leopard, mamba, serpent and original sin). Nebu realizes that he has been betrayed again. Wearily he says: ' "There was no leopard." (p. 78.) But, clearly, there was: no literal leopard, but a powerful instance of evil qualities the leopard symbolically represents.

The emotional heart of the novel is the relationship between Nebu and Toto. Toto is not only physically deformed; psychologically and morally he is a cripple. He has never known a mother, and his father has been incredibly malicious. Toto's physical deformity has set him apart from other children, and he reveals his insecurity in over-reaction: ' "It is I who will not play with them, you black fool!" he shrieked at Nebu.' (p. 50.) A potential killer, he is deceitful, willing to feign piety or love according to the moment's need; like the cat's paw he is 'the killer' that can seem 'sheathed and innocuous'. (p. 60.) 'The toto is false as a worm's skull.' (p. 100.) He is malignant, hateful at the core, unredeemed by the fact that he too can be made to suffer. In the American version of *The Leopard* Nebu sums him up explicitly: 'He hated so deeply that he would rather see his true father die than live himself.'[4] Toto is a sadist. He has enjoyed watching the house cat break the back of a mouse: 'The boy shivered deliciously remembering. . . .' (p. 60.) (But the memory prefigures his own death, struck down by a larger cat.) (p. 103.) Toto enjoys the sight of pain. He is disappointed that Nebu is so impassive: 'Suffering unmoved just like the dog long ago. And he was furious at Nebu for not exposing the pain. What thrill was there if it was not exposed?' (p. 74.) He was happier with the stout Somali woman who used to lift him up and down stairs. ' "We got along famously," ' he tells Nebu. ' "She never reported me to my father but she often cried. Her face was not cut from lumber, as was the dog's and yours." ' (p. 94.)

Cruel and deceitful as Toto is – 'false all through' (p. 94) – Nebu is bound to him in love and duty. Though relentlessly provoked, Nebu never rejects his son. Toto's most cruel betrayal is his pre-

[4] Victor Stafford Reid, *The Leopard* with an introduction by Gregory Rigsby (Collier Books, New York, 1971), p. 45. This edition is based on the edition published by The Viking Press, New York, 1958. There are many differences between the British and American versions. Some of the differences are important.

tence of returning Nebu's love (pp. 100—1.) Nebu recognizes Toto as part of himself, a penance gift enhanced in value when the child speaks Kikuyu and, though keenest on the predators, seems to have intimate knowledge of the natural world.

By trickery Toto manages to be carried first by Gibson and then by Nebu, his white 'father' and his black. Toto, the 'grey' mulatto, is the white man's burden and the black's; the white man hates him and plans to slit his throat; the black man loves him as a father and protects him dutifully.

Many readers have felt an allegorical dimension in the novel and particularly in the Nebu-Toto relationship. 'It would not be fanciful to see the half-bwana as a West Indian, having two fathers, the dead European . . . and the dying African.'[5] 'The Leopard is in its finest aspect a parable on the relationship between alienated West Indian and embarrassing African ancestry.'[6] 'Toto is symbolic of all cultures produced by a meeting of civilizations, whether in the Caribbean, or in Africa or India.'[7] Each of these judgments can be supported in detail. But Reid is anxious that readers also retain an awareness of the novel in its broadest significance, as it examines the ebb and flow of love and hate, between groups, between individuals and within a single person. In exploring a specific situation, Reid wishes to make us feel some human truths not limited by space and time.

The Leopard is set in 'a land . . . of impenetrable thickets and hinged valleys so vast you could lose the world's sins in them.' (p. 8.) Yet that land is Kenya; and Nebu is a black African, half-Kikuyu, half-Masai, represented in terms which relate him to Negro sculpture and the artistic currency of Negritude. Reid's The Leopard was the first West Indian novel in English set in Africa. But, when he wrote the book Reid had not yet visited any part of

[5] O. R. Dathorne, 'Africa in the Literature of the West Indies', The Journal of Commonwealth Literature No. 1, September 1965, p. 112.

[6] Kenneth Ramchand, The West Indian Novel and its Background (Faber & Faber, London, 1970), p. 159.

[7] Louis James, The Islands in Between ed. Louis James (Oxford University Press, Oxford, 1968), p. 70.

that continent. What is celebrated, with consummate craft, is an Africa of the mind, furnished with the names of trees and with details of ancestral custom.

The plot has many improbabilities, but they are hardly felt as a problem. A review in *Time*[8] put it well: 'What author Reid has done is to give his story the quality of near myth to make the horror understandable. ... Unashamedly contrived, his book is quite simply a brief imaginative triumph.' We accept the co-incidence that the white man Nebu trails should turn out to be Bwana Gibson, the one white man Nebu's morality forbids him to kill. It is a little harder to accept that although Gibson recognizes the boy as part-black the white community in general evidently does not; and that Gibson nurses his malicious intent against Toto for so many years while pretending to be his father. But, as Barrie Davies has observed: 'One feels that the "realistic" appeal here has as little relevance as the plot of *The Winter's Tale* to the final effect.'[9]

We are carried forward by a sensuous poetic prose of artful simplicity. Two very searching critics, Kenneth Ramchand and Mark Kinkead-Weekes, separately, have identified what they deem moments of stylistic collapse lying side by side with undeniable achievement; what Ramchand calls 'a mixture of over-writing with superb imaginative effects.'[10] Their analyses help us to appreciate the detail of Reid's power; not all their strictures seem justified. Both are, for example, severely critical of pp. 11–13 and p. 14. 'It is clear,' writes Ramchand, 'that Reid wants us to see this event as a re-enactment of the dance by Nebu and the "joyous uproar" of the earth under the rains, fertilization of the woman by mystic force of Nebu. But what we actually read through the clichés is an un-original description of sex on a stormy day.'[11] Kinkead-Weekes observes: 'The scene, after all, *is* a cliché; and that is sad, because it

[8] April 14, 1958.
[9] *World Literature Written in English* Vol. 11 No. 2, November 1972, p. 83.
[10] Ramchand, op. cit., p. 155.
[11] ibid., p. 157.

had promised so much more than sex in a storm with the extra twist of negritudinist wish-fulfilment . . . the language, sensitive index to the quality of imagination, shows how self-indulgence replaces the exploration of the artist.'[12] But one man's 'self-indulgence' is another's 'exploration'. Many readers – particularly black readers, sharing perhaps Reid's 'negritudinist wish-fulfilment' – have been enthralled even by those pages.

Kinkead-Weekes's subtle commentary on *The Leopard* is indispensable critical reading. But, overconfident in his inferences about the mind of the author, he assumes that Reid is largely unaware of what his language is doing. 'What we find ourselves involved with by the end of the third chapter is a struggle between two very different qualities of imagination, one indulgent and reductive, the other probing and exploratory . . . locked in Reid's mind below the level of conscious awareness . . .'[13] But it is by no means clear that Reid is not conscious of varying tendencies in the work (though he would no doubt describe them differently). Told mainly from the point of view of a Mau Mau guerrilla, *The Leopard* celebrates Nebu's black culture, his negritude, and powerfully expresses the Mau Mau's generalized hatred of whites; it also explores Nebu's humanity, of which the negritude and the hatred are only elements. In his account of the work, Kinkead-Weekes assumes that (racial) hatred is necessarily something to struggle internally against, to grow beyond; this is why he is disappointed by the final triumphant murder. Reid's novel, on the other hand, assumes that hatred can be justified in a war of liberation, and that a commitment to racial violence (in war) can co-exist with humane qualities.[14] '*Why cannot the white man understand?*' asks Nebu. (p. 25.) What is to be understood, *The Leopard* implies, is that the black

[12] *20th Century Studies* No. 10, 1973, p. 39.
[13] ibid., pp. 40–41.
[14] cf. 'Violence in order to change an intolerable, unjust social order is not savagery: it purifies man. Violence to protect and preserve an unjust, oppressive social order is criminal, and diminishes man.' Ngugi wa Thiong'o, 'Mau Mau, Violence and Culture', *Homecoming* (Heinemann, London, 1972) p. 28.

man is human; no worse – but also, alas, no better – than the white.

At the very beginning of the book we are reminded that cruelty and violence are human failings not confined to blacks. The Mau Mau attack on the Loman farm is imaged as 'a puff of lethal dust'. (p. 4.) Mau Mau wickedness seems trivial when set against the bombing of Hiroshima and Nagasaki.

Mervyn Morris
Department of English,
University of the West Indies,
Jamaica.

FURTHER READING
See page 109

PART ONE

1

Thirty were in the band which hit the Loman farm before daybreak. They slew all in the household and looted it of food, guns and ammunition and vanished into the bush again, and nobody shouted 'There they go!' because it was a sweet time for them to strike, when the morning ebb had drained the vigilance from the beleaguered settlers. But the looters found only three rifles.

Now three rifles were not enough to arm the gunless ones, so Nebu, who had joined General Koko's camp just four forays before, went without a rifle. And, puzzled at his constant ill luck, he now ran in the wake of his fellows as they entered the forest behind the farmhouse. Once among the trees, the troop took up the swinging trot which would put some twenty miles behind them by the time the raid was discovered by the morning patrol from Nairobi.

You would have noticed how the unshod black feet fell absolutely only upon those parts of the trail that were hard as stone after the long drought; and how they ran with their elbow devotedly glued to their ribs so as to shed no green leaves from the trees for the sharp-eyed police trackers to see. They ran in a tunnel of safety. They ran into a stream in a splashing commotion that quietened as the long line snaked into the middle, where the water rose to their armpits. Rifles held high above their heads, they breasted downstream for a mile to mystify the police dogs which would soon be nosing forth from the farm. They left the water by swinging up into the limbs of a squat, wide-spreading mango, going over from tree to tree as you cross the roofs in a city, and when they took to earth again they were half a mile away from the stream. A few colobus monkeys woke high in the trees and hugged their neighbours in beady-eyed, teeth-exposed chatter concerning the ghostly line moving along the forest floor underneath, and subsided when they had passed, and that was all. Just a puff of lethal dust that had by pure chance carried over the Loman farm.

2

Now Nebu thought and thought on his bad luck and found nothing to justify it. For in the troop he had played his part well, silencing a stubborn black servant with a thrust of his spear and providing cover for those whom Koko had chosen to perform the beautiful thing on the settler, his wife and whip-wielding overseer. But when afterwards they searched the house, only three rifles and many bullets.

Oh, it took only a mile to want, but it took ten miles to obtain. A man could in his green time gather a hutful of needs in the crown of his head and force them crosswise and downwards through his body until he grew heavy with it, but nothing would come until the time was ripe. Yet it was true that a man needed a rifle to fight the pink-cheek soldiers.

All of them possessed all sorts of wonderful weapons to stay out of sight and pick you off with ease. If you got close enough up to them, then it could be the duty of your knife. Some Kikuyus who had done this splendid thing spoke of how beautiful the white men became when they saw the panga purse its mouth to kiss their throats. But it was only at a great sacrifice that you could get up close.

At a sign from Koko, who was leading, they sank softly. Elephant grass grew thickly in that clearing up ahead, a fine place for an ambush. With eyes and noses and ears, they peeled back every root of the clearing and rose only when they had proved it innocent of enemies: this was when, at Koko's signal, Nebu sent two swift arrows into the grass from his wanderobo bow. A flight of plovers lifted from the grass, but it was the time for plovers to fly and s⊕ nobody had the gut-shrink. Yet they were wary when they rose, fo the English had become good bushmen since the Emergency an⊕ were hitting them with their own tactics often.

In bone and flesh Nebu felt sound, but the rebuff to his spirit b⊕ the elusive rifle was real as an aching cavity. Each time that the⊕ broke camp and headed south for their old Kikuyu land, it ha⊕ seemed to him the Great One would relent and give to him what hi shoulders and his fingers craved: the wood and iron of a rifle buil⊕ to snuggle into your shoulder and to curl your fingers around an⊕ gently squeeze. But it was not to be.

Mid-morning they halted by a stream and ate baked sweet po tatoes large as footballs and drank the limpid liquid that hissed an⊕ gurgled into their mouths. They joked about the overseer whom⊕ they had tied to the gatepost while they looted the place and did al⊕ they did to his master right before his eyes so that he would se⊕ what they would do to him. Koko, the leader, who called himsel⊕ General Koko, said the overseer had been beautiful when the⊕ stopped at the gatepost as they were leaving.

On again they ran like dark blue wraiths through the tangle⊕ loops of lianas wrapping as in rich laces gone shabby the straigh⊕ up trunks of cedars and tall pruans. They turned at the base of ⊕ magnificent copper-coloured boulder and plunged up a slope o⊕ shale. And where the land beyond the shale commenced to fatte⊕ up again for more forests, in a small cup of soil-drift formed in hollow of the shale Nebu saw the imprint.

It was the imprint of a white man's boot, a thickly studded on⊕ such as the settlers wore on their farms. Nebu, running in the rea⊕ dropped delicately to his haunches while the band ran on.

The imprint was well indented at the heel. The heel had sunke⊕ a good quarter of an inch into the cup. Nebu put his finger dow⊕ but did not touch the print. The finger traced the outline in the ai⊕ Uncannily, he was singing, although no sound issued from his lip⊕ The indrawn mask of a face tilted sharply up and he saw where th⊕ white man had stepped on harder ground after his single mistak⊕

6

But, farther up, the Negro's eyes marked the passage of the man into the bush, by the improbable bend of a twig, the dank underside of a skidded pebble, loose earth a toe-cap had sent scudding to the hard-packed root of a silk-oak.

A white hunter perhaps, or a lost settler. He carried a pack, a heavy one, for see the imprint of the heel; and a pack meant many valuable articles. But the noblest of these would be a rifle.

It had all been willed by the Great One who had seen Nebu's needs.

He stood upright again and looked all about him on land, and up at the wheelings of vultures and a tawny eagle crossing his patch of sky like the flick of a wrist. Sunlight in shafts ploughed into the earth, pressing up into his nostrils the smells of the bitter purity of the womb where coal was smelted into diamonds. Nebu tightened the thong holding the panga about his waist. The great wanderobo bow was secure and comfortable at his back. The seven-foot spear at his side was snug as a good wife on a cold night. He buttoned the old pea-jacket across his chest. The white man's trail bore upwards. The Kikuyu began to follow it.

3

From the mountain called Kenya (which has given the name to all the land) to the mountain called Ngong, and beyond it, is Kikuyu land. It is a land of immense folds and rolling parks; of water and forest and game; of impenetrable thickets and hinged valleys so vast you could lose the world's sins in them.

The wind is hot and dry when it enters the continent at Mombasa; but it cools when it reaches the highlands and they say it is like summer in Kent.

There are buffaloes and lions and rhinos and leopards and antelopes in the forests; great herds of eland and zebra, of wildebeest and giraffe roam the open parks.

In March, or sometimes in April, the long rains come, impregnating the earth with frightening fecundity, and the ancient wounds spread their lips again and new shoots spring from them.

It is a rich land: rich in humus and equally rich in hate, for all men crave it. Know, therefore, it is a land of feud: for the white challenger wants to conquer it, and the black man to keep it.

But none of the white men and few of the black understand it, or cope with it. Nor do any of the noble beasts, the lion or the rhino or the bull buffalo. Only the leopard understands it, for he avoids the strong and eats the wounded and the weak.

*

The trail was two or three days old, so Nebu knew that for now he could follow with speed and be unworried about caution. But his

8

speed must be tuned to his strength too! For when the time came for close stalking he must be fit and capable of closing with the quarry. He had all this carefully written inside his head, for it was the law.

In about six hours the light in the forest could grow too small for tracking. He could therefore run fast for these six hours, sleep very soundly and safely tonight in a high crotch of a tree, and run fast again all day tomorrow. The next day would be the time for stalking. He had it in his head as precisely as you or I would obtain the schedule from a railway time-table.

It was not long before he knew that the man he followed was no hunter; for he not only walked in the wrong places, but frequently stumbled. The bush was no place for white men who stumbled. He had even walked straight across a clearing where it was un-mistakable that a lioness and three cubs often lay about. Any toto old enough to walk would have smelled the place and carefully avoided it. Maybe it was a settler, but these went for walks in Nairobi, or did their stumblings at a night-time ngoma with the beautiful and conveniently unfertile Masai women.

Nebu knew the coffee-farming gentry very well. He had been a retainer in one of the stone houses on the Kenya slope built where his fathers had once herded their cattle. And as he raced forward, the quiver slapping at his hip, his eyes relentlessly reeling off each scuff of a boot, each rough brush of the white man's leather trousers against the bark of a tree, he was remembering.

He had come out of the bush after the Kaffir pox had decimated his tribe, a muscled, ebony youth of seventeen, and had wandered into the motor road and straight into the truck of Mulvaney, Bwana Gibson's white overseer, who had been looking for hands for the farm (five shillings a head for a bonus).

'Young ones, Mulvaney, those we can break in easily,' Gibson had told him. 'The older Kikes are too set in their bush ways. You get no work out of them after they have earned enough to buy themselves a snorter of palm wine. And do you know they resent us? Some of those oldsters wouldn't mind cutting our throats. Do you know those niggers called us squatters?'

'Squatters!' Bwana Gibson choked on the fury of recalling sweat and short commons, the pains that used to knot his bowels when the rains were late or the nights so cold the coffee berries blighted, the dreams he had at nights: he was a woman and the bank in Nairobi that held his notes was a man-bank, pursuing him with that monstrous phallic pillar.

Nebu dug irrigation ditches and wrestled mule ploughs until Bwana Gibson went home on furlough and returned with a wife. The old lick-and-promise ways of his bachelor days ended therefore. And Nebu, a strapping youth, was plucked from the field and planted in the house to scrub floors and move things. The woman had a firm seat on horseback and a great deal of fluency in her walk. She was a very young wife for the bwana, half his age.

*

Nebu the African turned away from the past and hearkened to what the present had to tell him. The sinews at his thighs roped and eased in smooth retraction at each stride. The Lawgiver within his breast pumped steadily along. He breathed calm as Sunday. He paid no attention to whether he was hungry.

The land had lifted very quickly and now the tall junipers and eucalypti were pointing proudly, kings of the highlands. Stringy mountain mushrooms appeared in the thinning undergrowth. Highland deer flashed about, too fast to shoot on the run. He hoped for an automatic rifle. He hoped the white man would have fitted it with telescopic sights. The black men called them the 'woman-guns' because of the way they talked fast and all the time and cruel as the Kikuyu women. Nebu remembered the European policeman at the stockade in Kiambu whose joke was castrating captured Kikuyu. One night Koko went to Kiambu and took him from his bed to the women deep in the Wakamba territory whose men had been eunuched. Deftly the women kept the policeman alive for a week, but it became bad for the hunting. The game shied away from all that perimeter where the policeman's agony could be heard.

*

By those blackened stones at the foot of a clump of bamboos, it was clear that the pink-cheek had slept all night by his fire. His eyes raced beyond the stones and picked up the spoor again. The white fool travelled slowly, as if he had a week to breast the next ridge. A woman with child would have made better time. Gravely humming to himself, Nebu ran on, thinking that if the rifle had a web attachment it would be more comfortable than the leather strap, which would hurt on a long march. Koko, who had two rifles, said so. Koko said he needed two, as leader.

The season of the long rains was any day now, he could sniff the wet in the afternoon wind, but he would be up with his quarry before they came. The trail was fresh. It would be good sense, however, to draw in the reel as rapidly as he could, for sometimes the storms broke suddenly. The Msabu Gibson had not known how suddenly storms broke in Africa. For she had been in Africa less than a year, on the day.

The day Bwana Gibson had gone off in the jeep early for Nairobi, where he had a seat in the Legislative Council, and his lady rode out for the field. Nebu the houseboy had swept and mopped the drawing-room, of cut stone walls and mahogany floors, and had rubbed the tanned alligator skin pegged out above the fireplace. He jockeyed the squeegee into the dining-room, the leaden foot stubborn and stiffly bumping along the narrow boards. He did the dining-room and headed for the largest room in the house, the main bedroom.

It was hot work working in the sodden pressures built up by the imminent rains; and Nebu succumbed to the heat and removed the red monkey-jacket. From this to tossing aside the foolish red fez and finally the white shorts was the matter of a flip of the head and

11

a fumble at the fly. The sweat prickled up hot and damp at every pore. He pushed open the heavy jalousies at the window and at that moment it seemed to Nebu as if the hot, sleepy earth breathed a gigantic, unceasing sigh. He stood stock-still at the window as the freshening breeze pushed through the trees and laid the yard corn on its ears, rolled across the lawns and flung the curtains stiffly into the room.

Vast, cold, furry hands instantly clamped themselves on every inch of his wet, naked body. He shivered violently at the first touch and then the bush flesh, that knew the elements with the primary acquaintance of a forest tree, accepted the wind with a gust of soft laughter. His head arrogantly cocked back on the column of ebony throat, Nebu laughed mirthfully. Miles away he heard the swiftly growing roar of the rain as it exploded on the sounding-board of this wide and cushioned land. Then the flood struck down on the trees outside and the house fell on his ears.

Nebu flung the squeegee away from him, opened his arms wide and bellowed laughter into the darkly wet void which his land had become. And suddenly it was a ngoma, but a ngoma that not the wisest master dancer among the Somali or the Masai or the Kikuyu could conceive. For the thunder of the rains was the drums, the whistle of the wind was the pipes, and although he was the only dancer at this ngoma, he was all the tribes in all the land from the borders of Ethiopia and Uganda to beyond mighty Kilimanjaro.

He danced full of power and able to perform impossible feats of agility in time to the rhythm of the rain-drums. The wind blowing on his nudity was the sweet-skinned girl whom the elders of the tribe had chosen for him at that half-forgotten Dance of Puberty when he had proved his maleness. Outside the windows the earth was in a joyous uproar beneat the rape of the long rains. The rain found all its hollows and embraced the hillocks. It soaked the trees to the roots.

Nebu danced nude, narrow-hipped, the strong calves and plough-widened shoulders like dark old wine catching what light there was about. In an odd way as he glided, a tiger grace to his flanks, he

12

seemed to claim the room: running his hand over the bedsheets, touching with his finger-tips the things of hers on the dresser, the lacy small clothes thrown on a chair – and then his dream world lurched. Nebu hooked his head round and stared into the eyes of the woman.

She had ridden in through the rainstorm and her clothes were soaked and clung to her horsewoman's body so that she was all long flat legs and shoulder hollows, and breasts proud as Babylon. The water-stiffened felt hat was in her hand. Brown hair flecked with water tumbled to her shoulders. The black, posed catlike on his sprung knees, was sculptured in hard, young manhood. With the tip of her tongue, the msabu touched the rainwater on her lips.

*

The incline sharpened as hills do before they meet a plateau. Nebu dropped back into the hill man's style, the legs swivelled outwards and cut back in a half-circle that added up to a huge stride without great muscular effort, storing his strength. Up on the plateau, he raced forward again. He took a guava from the knapsack and broke it, holding the halves in his cupped fingers to suck as he ran.

By tomorrow he should be up with the white man. Clearly the white man was an infant in the bush. He used a compass to tell him the way back to his camp, yet even the stupidest sheep, no matter how widely he grazed, knew the direction back to the fold. A good way to punish the white man would be to take him deep into the bush and turn him loose, without compass, a bow and spear. He would surely die. Just as they took the black man into their towns and made him lose direction by rolling him in their gutters and he never could find his way into the bush again. But this one was his, he would make him beautiful by tomorrow. It was ordained.

The lives of the children of the Great One were as ordained as the Nyeri's. The Nyeri rose in the mountain and rolled powerfully every mile, but its strength was a joke, for in the end it was nothing. For after it had flashed its teeth into boulders huge as twenty houses and wiped out whole villages, after all this anger, did it not end in the sea? As was ordained. So, men.

Women had the wisdom of the earth, which provided food for thorns and for the beautiful pine, for lion and lamb, and never lost. The lion ate the lamb who ate the grass which had the lion in the end.

And even where nightly she was wounded by men, she filled the wound with growth. This land, his Africa, was a woman: For look how soon after the rifts were scoured to sand by the rain, grasses grew in them.

*

And even now he remembered the rough thrusts of the msabu's hips when she fought for him to fill her, using the rich language of her body to talk away his fears. And the unfumble of her fingers opening the blouse to offer and offer. Planting, blooming and bursting while the rain lashed in at the window. Meanwhile in Mombasa, in the narrow cobbled streets built by the early Arab conquerors, the Negro policemen commenced evacuating the children of the English soldiers from a flooded schoolroom.

4

he pink one ahead is a fool as all the pink ones are fools, the black
aid to himself next morning as he ran arrogantly braced on his
eels, the legs scissoring under the wedge-shaped torso. The blue-
lack skin gleamed with health, the mask face had no expression.
Ie had shed the old pea-jacket, tying the sleeves about his waist so
hat it hung down his hips like a kilt.

Nebu had slept well. There had been a rabbit for supper, cooked
etween heated stones over a fire that had no smoke. Then he had
urled in the crotch of a tree and had woken at the first light and
icked up the trail. Now the sun was curving into the first quarter,
he sky immense and blue and the tree-tops glinting. Proudly he
hought how he had taken the trail at the cold end yesterday and
ad run it into warmth. By tomorrow it should be hot under his
eet. The white man was slow, the signs told him.

The land was a book you learnt to read.

Men, beasts, fowls, moonrise, the shape of trees were all ex-
lained in the book.

And only when you had learnt all about the lacerated paths the
rimitives had come by could you widen them, or pave them, or
ut up filling-stations in them.

*

All the pink ones are fools, the black said to himself as he sped on
is mission. *They come in and laugh at our god and say to us: 'Beat
o more drums to your god, already he is deaf.'* Then they bring

their own god whom they must smoke out with incense or light candles to see. They are as few as a handful of pebbles, yet they say to us who number as the sands at Kilindini: 'Stay in your pocket of a Reserve unless we need you to plant our coffee.' Yet such fools would walk as lords of our land.

Great One, give us long knives.

He ran across a narrow neck of marshland on a mat of papyrus which had been flattened by his clumsy quarry. His eyes gleamed cruelly.

This one must be fat and panting beneath his burden of leather boots and tins of sardines. But he thought of the pack with affection for in it would be a rifle. The rifle had made gods of the white men. He would be proud to slay this one and would carefully put the deed into song and sing to his grandchildren when he grew old. He would not have been proud to slay Bwana Gibson, for he had wronged that one. He had never done it with the msabu again.

But she had fixed a fierce tenderness in him and he would have fought lions with his hands for the white woman. With hauteur, Nebu reflected that the sun had the same tenderness for the tiniest flower in the bush and sometimes sent a finger through the thicket to touch it.

One morning, Bwana Gibson had entered the breakfast room and seen him place the bowl of double zinnias at her place and something about his hands on the bowl must have disturbed the bwana, for he had pushed it aside and, laughing irritably, said: 'You know, your Kikuyu boy fairly worships you, Edith. The way he hovers about you.' And she had quietly replied: 'I know.' Leaving Bwana Gibson nothing to do but go on with his breakfast and after a while mumble into his spoon: 'You've got to be careful of them. There's some trouble brewing in Nairobi. Some terrorist gang springing up.'

And then there had been nothing more about it, for everyone was concerned with the outbreak in Nairobi. Nothing more until the night of the storm when the cedars and the chestnuts and the olives had howled and wept and died of broken backs, and rivers had raged over what had been roads, and the bwana went mad.

*

Nebu dug in his heel and braced to a frozen halt. He stood quite still after the panga was gathered in his hand.

From the top of a boulder, a leopard had bounded into the clearing and stood sideways, straddling the trail, the head turned towards the black. The blade breathed in Nebu's hand, a living thing, and he was bent as a bow. The hunter fixing yellow eyes unwaveringly on Nebu, slowly exposed its teeth. The demoniac head never left off pointing at Nebu while the heavy tail lashed slowly. Nebu had the chill feeling that the leopard was learning his image. Suddenly it leaped into the bush, wanton cruelty in every wicked line, and the path was clear. Nebu let go of the rocks he had been breathing in.

Unaccountably, the evil slew of the beast's head had reminded him of Bwana Gibson; the night the bwana had become an animal, shrieking and battering-in the flower face of the msabu as she lay spent and weak after the birth while Nebu crouched in the storm outside and peered in at them through the window.

*

It was chilly in the afternoon high up on the slopes. The air smote Nebu running along an exposed ridge and he put on again the old pea-jacket. The wool warmed his shoulders. Heath grass waved cobs around his feet and there were blackberries about. The long legs were pistons below the flat, functional abdomen. He had run all day, slaking his thirst at waterholes, and now he was tingling with it. He could smell it near, smell it in tomorrow. Perhaps even by sunset he would be up with the white man, for the white man was slow as a cow.

Now it is a fact that Nebu was hurrying towards a murder, but it did not appear in that way to him at all. To him, he was stalking a dangerous man-animal. An animal you could never get upwind of, for he had no upwind nor downwind. He was a gun: he hid a mile away behind a tree and slew you. And you were able to hate him as you could never hate a lion, for a lion never ignored your customs, nor laughed at them. A lion was even willing to share his land with you, provided you took the day and allowed him abroad at night.

A stone, unseen under the moss, raked the sole of his right foot and while he ran he listened to what the injured foot had to say. His body was a tool he frequently used to the limit these days and a flaw could hamper him fatally. And it was not only the danger of stalking a gunman on a lame foot, but Nebu was looking to the time when he re-entered Koko's camp bearing the trophies of his dead foe. He should be upright then as a young palm. General Koko was all for walking upright. Koko, who had lived in the white man's cities, said that the blacks there affected a walk of bowed heads and shoulders so as to indicate that they were yoke-worthy.

'Have nothing to do with the white man – except to make him beautiful,' Koko frequently raved, 'and he is only beautiful when he dies of Mau Mau!'

Koko also said: 'When they do not humiliate you, my brothers, they laugh at you. Are you giraffes or monkeys that they should laugh at you?'

Nebu had been (only once) to an Adult Education class at Kiambu and had seen some tribal elders stuttering over the words in the white man's book while a couple of young white overseers outside the hut grinned in at the window. And when Nebu had remembered the wine-skin of words which would pour from the mouths of those elders at a tribal council, words whose whispers were the winds combing the heads of the taller pines, or thunder at the commencement of the seasons, or the sweet poetry of his people singing at the spring ngoma, he had turned to look at the young overseers, the wish to torture bright in his eyes.

Who saw our land in the morning, from Kilindini to where the snow flies? Nebu the warrior sang in his head and along his veins as he ran. *Great Spirit, give us long knives.*

*

He brought down a deer during the evening's soft rush of small game hurrying to cover before the big cats came out. He fetched the carcass into the clearing through which the white man's trail ran, and crouched by the bole of a dead acacia to make a fire and skin it. And the curve of his back grew rigid as he stared at what he saw down there.

For amidst the welter of crushed leaves and broken twigs that marked the blundering way of his quarry Nebu clearly saw the print of a boot – a woman's boot. The boot had slid from the rib of a wet leaf and touched lightly in the earth, but it rang a thunderclap in the head of the black.

Eyes, Nebu cried silently, *where have you been since yesterday, Nose, why have you caught none of the scents which the women of the pink-skins bathe their bodies in?*

Angry and ashamed, Nebu silently rebuked the members that had failed him.

Pluck yourselves out, eyes.

Fall away, useless nose.

He crouched above the imprint of the boot, brooding, huddled over, deadly somehow.

*

And early next morning, before the dew had dried on the pale-bellied mogan grass, the white man was in his eyes.

5

The white man was in his eyes there behind the torn boma where the smoke rose. He had camped on the edge of a stream, a stream that stumbled over too many rocks; it needed a knock on the head to keep it quiet. But the man was a baby, a pink baby who owned a gun. For who would camp by a noisy stream that would hide the approach of your enemy?

The Kikuyu had run early and had come up with the camp soon after daybreak. He had slipped in closer, preparing for a quick rush, when he remembered that the slowest of white men were salty with their guns. He was stumped for an instant until recollection of the white man's finickings when he was on safari with his woman brought grave laughter into his head. He would let the white man come to him. So he wriggled through the grass until he was downstream of the camp.

Now all he had to do was to wait. And he had all the fearsome patience of his land: of the cats waiting like portraits; of maimed trees waiting to flourish when the axeman had gone.

His cheek rested on the seven-foot spear extended on the ground. He had unsheathed the panga. All his muscles relaxed, deliciously quiet. Only his brain was alive in unrelated fragments.

Koko is asking anxiously these days: 'Is there much killing in Dagoreti? Much death in N'drobo? In Chipalungu? Nairobi?'

How can a man keep sheep these landless days with the rains turning more and more into the mountains?

Do the yellow bamboos bloom better in spring or autumn? Huts

*should be built of bamboo and thatched with juniper, and sleep
would be deep and scented.*

Such fragments.

The fog was slow fog in this morning without wind, but the sun
was vigorous higher up and day stood on the top of the trees. As
the sunlight strengthened, some of the fog tore away in great
hinged sweeps. A man on safari should be out and doing.

But perhaps he is doing his hunting on the belly of his woman,
Nebu thought. It had been so in the Ngong hills when Bwana
Gibson had taken his bride on safari. The tent flaps had hung down
into the high morning, and when you wandered near you heard the
buffalo lappings. And Nebu had averted his head when later the
red-faced bwana emerged grumpy and exhausted, and from
the cerval-cat eyes of the woman.

A shaft of smoke shot up behind the boma when the coffee-pot
was removed from the fire. Now the woman would be pouring for
her lord and they would be sitting together, nursing the warm cups
in their hands. The African lay full-length, listening to the ancient
hymns inside the earth. A cricket shrilled at the bottom of a stone
and he heard the beat of a beetle's bony wings. A small thing
wriggled through the grass and the stalks sawed impatiently to be
upright again. He had the bull-thonged bow with an arrow in it
beside him, but he hoped to use the knife. Arrows whistled and
warned. The white man's guns never warned.

All the great hunters of his land gave warning, except the
leopard and the white man. Oh, look now. The forests saw the
coming of the wind when the sky put on cloaks and unsheathed
the lightning. The small boar knew the lion was loose when the
shadows deepened under the trees. The earth knew surely in what
month would come the teeth of the long rains. But the bwanas stole
farms without a wink, farms a day's journey to cross. The bwana,
like the leopard, was a lesser cat: he was king of neither forest nor
plain. He slew sneaking, he killed the wounded and the weak. *The
bwanas come from other lands, rich lands of which they boast.*

Why don't they return and leave to us our land which they revile and ridicule?

All these things Nebu thought and there was too much gravity in his hate for it to be hate, more; it was the tragedy of a truth, so simply constructed that only saints should build it or live in it. Both sides were full of sinners.

6

And the Great One dug the white man in his bowels and made him rise from beside his woman and go off to find a place of privacy downstream, grunting like an ill-humoured pig at the insecure stones and the soft sands of the river bed which twisted his ankles. Nebu, hidden in the grass, listened to his approach, singing the death song deep inside him, his big body twitching, learning through an ear pressed to the ground what the earth told him in the squeak of grass, the crush of pebbles, the angry whine of discommoded insects: the time when he should rise and kill.

He read the story of the bwana's approach and sent it down into the springy thigh muscles and along the arm that held down the panga flat in the grass. *The fat pig is ready*, at last said the stones and the sawing grass. The black reared to his feet and the hand holding the knife flew back. But, for a winking instant, the assault was stayed.

For the bwana whose mouth took that whistling inrush of air, whose torn eyes poured their whites down the disordered face, was Bwana Gibson.

Nebu turned into stone for a year. It took all that time for Bwana Gibson's rifle to come up before he was quickened into flesh again and drove in the knife. He reeled away from the flash of the rifle and hit the earth with a hard bump.

*

Hear me, Great Spirit, he cried exultantly even as the white man's bullet smote him, *all the plains are ours, the Plains of Athi, at the foot of Lord Kenya, on which the white man built his cities.*

And the mountains are ours. And the rivers. And the forests. And the animals are ours.

By right of possession. By right of coveting no other land beyond Kikuyu. And those who enter our land must obey our right, or be destroyed as Thou, Great Spirit, destroyest those foolish trees who do now bow to Thy wind.

*

Nebu held the holes in his side and struggled to his haunches. The blood trickled out of both mouths of the wound, for the bullet had gone clear through. He pinched the holes shut in his fist. With the other hand he loosened earth to make a poultice. His face a mask of indifference, he removed his eyes from the wound and turned them on the bwana, who was babbling from the ground.

'She – ha-had – you a nigger ba-baby—'

Nebu, who knew lunacy, saw it in the clear, flawless eyes which were at odds with the tortured face. The bwana was foolishly wrestling with the panga. But it was buried too deeply in his chest. The face went placid, then it twisted, swam away, and returned with the muscles all broken up. *I have made him beautiful*, Nebu thought triumphantly.

'A – a – dam' freak – she had a – a – freak!' the bwana cried violently.

A man should go away with the poetry of ease on his tongue, the black thought. *Like a sapling going down in the quiet good-byes of leaves whispering; going down on a boon of wind that took it gently to earth. Not like an unwilling old tree, quarrelling inside its rotten bole, writhing and shrieking all the way as it fell, destroying right and left the young ones of the forest.*

'—tol-told him about you. I – I – told the little grey mo-monkey about the – black ape who is – is his – father – just before I brought

24

– him – back – to the bush. *Ha, ha – you should have seen – his face!'*

The bwana's countenance turned sick in the midst of his laugh. A small area of pain exploded in Nebu's side as a tissue tore when he moved. The mask-face showed nothing as he looked coldly at the dying man. He waited for the pain to go from his side, gathering strength in his belly and thighs and knowing surely that soon he would tower to his feet and watch the bwana die. Gibson screwed his eyes shut and grimaced as the agony closed in. The black turned his own eyes inward and watched how the dark tide of pain would be lapping at the vitals of the bwana. The heat stored in his loins would be turning cold as the line of the tide edged nearer. Pain was very powerful. It was known to knead men into forms that would make a stone laugh. The bwana grunted and drew up his knees. The blood suddenly stained all his chest and appeared at his lips.

'*Nebu*—!' he shrieked. '*Black ape*—! I brought your son back to the bush so – he could – watch you die! Then – then I would have – slit his throat—!'

The bwana had no grace. Bwana Gibson had turned ugly, going away. The bitter waters had gathered at the root of his tongue and left no room for the sweet poetry of ease. It saddened one to hear it.

Soundlessly, his thoughts concealed behind the mask, Nebu sang the death song for Gibson. He died hard, worrying the blade like a dog with a bone, grunting and heaving as if he too would stand on his feet, as Nebu. The Kikuyu thought of dispatching him with a blow to the head, but decided against it. He would want to tell General Koko all about these moments of the bwana being made beautiful. He drew an arrogant breath. There was no pain. Gibson sleepily drew back his eyelids and looked at Nebu.

'Look – look at me, black swine,' he said softly. 'Dy-ing like a white man. Do you – see – me – begging?'

But neither would I, Nebu thought, gleaming black eyes in his pitiless face fixed like lights on the crumbling features. *Why cannot the white man understand?*

The bwana was going now, for sure. He had ceased to struggle.

The blood-wet ground was a door on which his knuckles kept tapping, tapping.

The white man has no understanding! cried the African angrily in his head, and swiftly stooped and wrenched out the blade.

It ended for Gibson in a rain of pain that made his ruined body jump for the knife. Slowly, while it sank back, Nebu reached for the rifle. He had it in his hand. Dew was on the barrel and it was cold. For the first time, he remembered the woman. He wheeled to slip for cover, and then he saw the boy.

7

Nebu bristled with weapons. In his left hand he carried the alien piece, the rifle. His right held the untidy sprout of the spear and panga and the wanderobo bow. He pushed his hands with all the weapons towards the boy and they looked at each other across them. The black, straight-boled as a good tree, bulked up, heels together. The boy stood crooked, one shoulder reaching higher.

There is no woman, the eyes of Nebu the Tracker said ashamedly. He looked the boy up and down and saw the crippled foot. The heel of the diminutive boot which touched the ground had made him think a white woman was in the safari. The eyes of Nebu the Tracker were ashamed.

My son has but one sound foot, the other is a twig. A yell of obscene laughter broke out inside him. He could hear it. It stopped.

The boy was thin and neat and grey. He had brown hair curling like smoke so that you could not see the ends. He never moved his eyes after they had stopped on Nebu; never looked beyond Nebu to the patch reddening on the ground. The black let down his weapon-filled hands and stood as an equal before the boy.

'How do you do?' the boy asked politely.

'The – bwana – is – weary,' Nebu observed, dredging up the long unused foreign words so that they trailed muddily in his throat. 'He is – gone – into the long sleep.'

The boy asked: 'Are you a Kikuyu?'

'Half,' Nebu said gravely. 'My mother was Masai.'

'You lie,' the boy said like a bwana. Nebu thought he could be the chief of police in Nairobi. 'The Masai never marry outside the tribe.'

It flinched the black, but he was on penance, for he had wronged the bwana who lay in the grass behind him. He had taken the bwana's woman. He said: 'I farm on my father's side and I am a hunter on my mother's side. I am half.'

The boy said: 'How do you stand comfortably like that? Can you ride a bicycle?'

There is much for you to learn, half-bwana. You may stand this way for a day when you are a herds-boy, with the sole of one foot clamped behind the knee of the other to hold you tall in guarding the grass against a leopard going on his belly into the herd. 'How do you go into the bush crippled in one foot? Do you fly like a bird above the trees?' Nebu asked.

The boy laughed pleasantly. 'My father carries me. My father is a fool. Mad as a March hare.'

The morning was hardening as birds woke and flew out to their businesses. Nebu stepped past the boy and, crouching and dodging from bush to bush, legged it swiftly towards the boma where the bwana had made camp. He dodged up the bank of the stream and came in around the end of the thorn fence. His nostrils dilated at the white smells. There was no woman.

There were two rubber ground-sheets still spread on the ground and a knapsack, a coffee-pot beside the fire, two cork helmets, one for a man and the other for a boy, an ammunition belt and nothing more. The boy hopped in behind him and went to the fire and sat down, favouring the lame foot in his lap.

'Why did you kill my father?' he asked Nebu. 'Because he is mad?'

'Your – father?'

The eyes of the boy went blank and the high shoulder twitched forward for him to lay a cheek on. He grinned boyishly at Nebu when sight returned to his eyes. The boy touched a pocket in the short jacket he wore. His brown eyes were brown doors, locking-in big and little secrets.

Paying penance was important to Nebu. It was the law. You could slay with easy conscience an enemy in warfare. But when you killed someone whom you had already wronged, for this you paid penance; by a dozen goats, or a cow and bullkin, or a favourite wife. But there was nothing he could pay Bwana Gibson with. All Kikuyu-land had been broken and thrown away. And to whom could he pay? The policemen in Nairobi? The Queen in England? The bwana had nobody, not even a son.

'This – you make a safari?' Nebu asked. 'You hunt?'

'He said we would hunt niggers for the bounty,' the boy lied. 'But he was quite mad. You ever heard of a hunter *carrying* a hunter?'

When you grow older, Nebu stated clearly and silently, *you will wear false teeth and no shoes. You are half a white man.*

'I am Nebu,' Nebu said. 'What do they call you?'

The grey face paled. 'Ne – you are Neb—'

And suddenly the boy shrank away and the high shoulder came up. He buried his face in the high shoulder and peered out at Nebu from under his arm.

He was hearing the music more frequently nowadays and it was no longer the dim strings at the bottom of the crocodile pool, muffled and wet, but the high, thin clarity which the little goat-men plucked on their instruments 'way up on top of the mountains of the moon.

The black was looking back at him. He ducked his head and peered craftily out again. That sharp nigger would pin him if he didn't watch out. *Careful*, wrote a hand on the brown doors of the boy's eyes and they swung shut again.

'Did – my fa-father speak back there?'

'No.' Nebu said the untruth quietly. 'The bwana was tired.'

The eyes regarded him slyly from their half-concealed place. Then the boy straightened and looked fully at the negro.

'I am the young bwana,' he said. 'Have a cup of tea.'

'Coffee,' Nebu said gravely, glancing at the coffee-pot. *We, the people of the Kikuyu, cleared the ground and ploughed it and plot-*

ted the cuttings that grew into this, Nebu sang in the deep as he placed the coffee-pot on the coals.

'You have come from Nairobi?'

'All the way from Nairobi,' the boy answered soberly, inspecting the clean leather sole that bottomed the shoe on the crippled foot. He looked up. 'I say, you do ask a lot of questions for a black.'

Nebu looked steadily at him until the brown eyes were taken off.

Whom do you pay to when there is nobody to collect? And what do you pay with when all your goats have been scattered? When there is nobody to collect, you pay to the tribe. That is the law from the Rift Valley to where the sun sets beyond the shoulder of Lord Kenya. In goats, or cattle, or woman. You paid in flesh, the law said, but Nebu had no flesh except his own bullet-torn body.

'Have your coffee, General Nebu,' the boy suggested.

Nebu dropped down and poured hot coffee into the white man's cup and drank noisily, thirstily, the mug of hot liquid that scalded his throat with all that goodness, aromatic, strengthening, filling his empty belly.

The boy looked up and cried explosively: 'No!'

Slashing his hand forward, he knocked the mug from the African's hand. Then the good foot kicked towards him with easy custom – the discarded tin that had contained the condensed milk. 'Keep that for your use.'

Nebu hoped desperately that the hate pulling him to his feet would go away; but it swept him up. He was blind and lonely with hate and he groped for the young stranger who had put out his eyes.

'No—!' the boy shouted so loudly it cracked his voice across. 'No – Nebu, *no!*'

The cry went in and Nebu halted his hands inches from the boy's jugular. He stared at the scared flutter of the pulse beneath the grey skin and at the sweat in the hollow at the base of the boy's neck where a blow from the edge of his hand would have divided it like a doll. The black slipped slowly back to his haunches, his shoulders narrowed.

'Li-like the pox – you could catch the bwana's madness from his cup just as you could catch the pox,' said the boy. He was still shaky and the strokes of his tongue lining his way out of the trouble were unsteady.

'I will use the bwana's cup,' Nebu said softly.

The brown doors in the boy's eyes closed without a click. 'Of course.'

*

The Negro rose and stalked up-river and went to the edge of the water. The wound in his side spoke to him. He breathed in deeply and it became quiet. He swallowed on a sort of shame at the weakness in a man that made him fool himself into believing that the false fire was true fire, that wine power was true power, that goats' ordure, being black, was diamonds. For half-bwana had not fooled him. He had glimpsed the brown doors closing and he knew that the boy was in accord about the bwana's cup only because he was the weaker. But was a man's door not meant to be closed? All men made their own stockades of habits and customs, and they never welcomed intruders. In the old, strapping days, who among the Somali had ever drunken from the Kikuyu's ceremonial bowl of calabash set on the shelf made from the olive? The strapping days when the moranis had walked on their heels and boasted of the number of hostile warriors they had made beautiful.

So, he excused the boy.

The stream rushed and fought small splashing battles over the rocks and ran hurriedly past the calms to fight farther downstream. Nebu turned back to the camp to retrieve his bow and hunt a fat little one for his food. Then he remembered that now he owned a rifle. He grew and grew into a giant, seven leagues tall.

8

The rifle was everything it had promised in his dreams to be. The stock was sweat-polished, the heel grooved for shoulders, a front sight seeing through which you cut the sky into neat segments; for an instant you held an eagle in the steel-framed windows; for a longer while you looked at a nob of cloud that could be parted from the sky by a squeeze of your finger. A godlike feeling. The thing balanced in your hand faultlessly, built for you from the commencement of time. It was such, you wanted to sing.

Nebu dropped the gun into his lap and wiped his forehead with the back of his hand. He could go to bed with such a gun. He lifted it again and sank his cheek to the cold metal of the barrel as he had seen Koko do and looked along the pure line to the end through which the bullets went. There was the top of a tree he could blow off, the head of a mountain he could shoot away, a wood-pigeon he could halt and shatter. He was gifted with destruction.

He looked down at the grey-skinned boy. He looked at him from the sound foot, up past the twig of the other uselessly thrown across the sound thigh, over the interlaced fingers to the petulant, heavy-lipped mouth and the brown eyes blank as tomorrow. *You, too, half-bwana*, Nebu thought, *could be broken quickly by the rifle.*

Nebu got to his feet and moved out of the camp. *A fat little one,* his hunger said, but the grand dreams had woken, bellowing in him that now he was lord of life and death. He almost ran for the bush.

9

And the bush was waiting and drew him in with a hundred thousand green arms in heat for him. He looked back over his shoulder when the branches of a wild banana clashed behind him and then he swam into the green cave. He held the rifle familiarly, so often had he held it in his dreams. Now he had it in is hand and it felt familiar. He walked exalted, he was of the salt of the earth.

But his head said: *Seek signs, Nebu*, and the part of him that was hunter broke free of the false thinking and began to note the fall of the land and the way the brush opened for the animal trail to the waterhole. The path had been pressed down by the great furry paws and the stomping ones of all the beasts who had gone down it to the drinking-place, immemorially. The black slipped swiftly along, his fingers working tightly on the hard virginity of the stock, the stock that sank here and there into the simple dimples of the Masai girl, and he thought how soon it would tongue out the boom of flame and be a big delicious woman declaring for him.

It was yet early for the morning drink and occasional lave of the small fat ones, the bush pig and the deer, the spurfowl and guinea-fowl, the antelope and the gazelle whose legs would snap like sparrows' but whose meat was fit for the kitchens of the Great Spirit. So Nebu made for a slight knoll one dozen feet from the edge of the waterhole and with quick slashes of the rifle butt cleared out a nest behind a screen of shrubbery and folded himself into it.

Generations of wild animals had with hooves and paws punished the earthen bank of the waterhole so it was giantly chipped and scarred like pottery knocked about. A frog jumped in the soupy water and launched forward, square-shouldered and high in front of the grey furrows it drew on the surface.

Behind his cover, Nebu was a dark legend waiting to come true. Excitement prickled sweatily from his pores and he wiped the palms of his hands on the pea-jacket. He found firm places for his elbows and now he was a dark river of stone anchored into the earth and he waited in impregnable, unyielding patience. He looked along the barrel again where the brave bullets would soon burst in a brilliant shower. He had learnt many things from the bwanas. He had learnt how with a small metal animal you could open a stolen can of peaches without disfiguring it on a rock; how with a key no larger than the hiding-places in the middle of his hand, he could unlock the stoutest iron door; how a pair of scissors could cut through tin as a knife through a slab of butter: all knowledge that was wonderful and overflowing in splendour. Most Kikuyus in the bush had never heard of such things. And the most wondrous of all was the metal animal he now held in his hand, the animal which the white man had mated out of his arithmetic and gunpowder and used to plough under his enemies, just as the Kikuyu ploughmen had done when they mated the buffalo and the bull and brought the strong and amenable half-buffalo. Now he had it and he would learn to use it. *Firm places for your elbows.* Koko, who had two rifles, had been emphatic about this.

*

The first to enter Nebu's sights was a spurfowl and her brood, scampering fearfully to one of the tributary pools which drained through a fold in the bank. He framed the sight on the old hen, and his indrawn, fatal eyes in the excited mosaics of his face were candles shooting up and down in a windy room. And then, inch by inch, he lowered the weapon and the arrogant head came up from the barrel.

The black lay coiled immobile in his nest while his mind became a half-lit battlefield in which ideas fought softly and died. A bush pig and an antelope and other food leaped from the forest to the

34

table around the waterhole and the sun thickened through the leaves, warm and yellow, flowing down the trunks. And he had this final thought: *It is unworthy of a morani.*

It was unworthy of a warrior that his unbloodied weapon should first be used on the fat little ones. Such a weapon was made for the royal lion, or the strong buffalo, or the sly, treacherous leopard who is schooled in ways of evading the powerful and going after the weak. So he rose to his feet and turned away from the waterhole and went into the bush. And he looked for spoor until mid-morning but found none that was fresh enough to draw him along, for he would not hunt far from camp: none until he had crossed the Valley of Smoking Skies, as he named it in his head because the dun clouds hung low, swinging between the hills like thick smoke.

It had a gorgeous floor of periwinkles and copper-red cineraria, and the loveliest tree in the wood grew there, the poetic podo, going up straight as a sunbeam for seventy feet and roofed in foliage green as Eden. And on a low branch of the wild fig whose tiny leaves shone like jewels three spear-lengths ahead of him Nebu saw the ugly evil waiting for him, disfiguring the beautiful valley, horrifying to him as a mamba coiled in a Communion cup. Trained to be still at the unexplained flutter of a leaf, the negro was a monolith in the sun.

His eyes took in the leopard on the branch, the narrow forehead that bore a curious resemblance to the serpent's, the puff-stitched mouth like a badly mended purse, the front paws neatly crossed before the face. But the brute was perfectly at ease, no cobra swell at the neck, no quiverings at the shoulder, and Nebu commenced to bring up the rifle, had it at his shoulder and bearing on the leopard. Then, his breathing securely locked away for the present, he began gently to squeeze the trigger as he had seen Koko do. But he squeezed for ever and ever and nothing happened, nothing exploded. The leopard lived, neat, inviolate.

Nebu released the spring of the trigger and pulled again, a little quicker this time, and at the dry click he did it again and again, but the white man's weapon would not speak for him. He jerked and tugged at the trigger, sweat piling on his forehead. He held it away and pulled. He looked down into the barrel and at the same time, at the risk of blowing off his head, jerked the trigger again. And in the silence, filled only with dry clicks, his heart leaped six houses. His bowels went mad and knotted themselves into a pain he never knew existed. The hills closed in and crushed him, broke the bones in his chest, broke all his bones, and when the dust of himself had blown away and the sun gave light, he saw that the leopard had gone. The fig tree and the valley were both empty, and he was heartsick and washed in sweat and doubt.

For it seemed that Ngai, the All-Seeing, had forsaken him. Ngai, the All-Seeing of the Kikuyu, who lived on the highest places of the land, on Kenya and Juja and Aberdare and Ngong, but was present in all the children of the Kikuyu, had departed from him. Five forays had been made on the white intruders and had failed to find a rifle, and when he had, finally, run a cold trail into blue heat, the rifle he had found would not speak for him. But he knew why he had failed. Crushed as he was into little pieces in the Valley of Smoking Skies, he knew why he had failed. Ngai had taught that the man who did wrong would not go unpunished, unless he paid in the material he most loved, flesh of his cattle or his woman. And it was two times he had wronged the Bwana Gibson and not once had he paid.

And then like trade winds rising, like the first crocus to blow, like the tawny pride of old wine that takes slowly until the sudden onslaught in the blood, knowledge of how he could pay the debt was understood in Nebu. He had flesh, the coin of blood payment, and he knew where he would find Bwana Gibson's tribe to whom the payment should be made. The bwanas were all of Nairobi, or Mombasa, or Fort Smith at Dagoreti, where the older Kikyus had put up their fortified villages and slain the first inrush of the English who had come with Milord Lugard. He would regain credit with the Great One.

Nebu commenced his return to the camp and the hole in his side awoke and shrieked all the way. When he stumbled into the boma the boy looked curiously at him.

10

The long rains arrived in the early afternoon. Nebu had been burying the bwana, putting him under, that the curse would go from the rifle. He dug the grave with his panga and gave up a couple of arrows to lie at the bwana's side, old things which he had been taught had virtue. He cast in the loose earth from the feet upward and finally threw dirt on the face. Then he wiped his hands free of dirt and knowledge of the bwana. The curse should go with that gesture. He heaved upright on his straight thin-muscled legs and the pain at his side was balled in a fist. He gasped and stood where he was until it flattened out. He turned his head away from the long rectangle at his feet and listened. He heard it. He heard the coming of the rain across the land, a clatter punctuated by heavy reports of thunder. He loped from there, making for the camp. The boy looked at his hands when he came in behind the boma, the first rains thumping down in lumps on his uncovered head.

'You have brought no game,' the boy said, his eyes on the black's hands. 'You are no good with a gun.'

Nebu dropped down and looked in at the open brown doors before they were quickly closed. He thought that in there he had seen a kind of laughter folded back like a weapon. But one did not show anger to a toto. The lion did not roar at a mouse.

'The Masai hunter has failed. Will the Kikuyu farmer now dig roots for our meal?'

Not even when the little mouse gnawed at him should the lion roar. The grey boy huddled farther into the shelter of the lean-to they had built above the ground-sheets. The mushroom drops had changed into the tremendous tears that would splash from the sky until the sun shone again. Nebu reached slowly for one of the sheets, his eyes on the boy. He saw the dim flare of his nostrils when he closed his fingers on the sheet and suddenly spilled it in the air, ridding it of water and fallen leaves. He drew it down in a cape over his head and shoulders and tied the laces across his middle. Snug as an egg, he gestured his thumb at the other sheet and rose. Slung on his back by the web attachment, the rifle conically pushed up the sheet. His wide-apart feet had been washed clean by the rain and showed the high-ridged bone shapes and the turn of the great toes that had crossed continents in bondage time and again. He looked a tall strange splinter from the past.

Nebu moved about, gathering items and putting them into a bundle. The boy asked in a high clear voice: 'Where are you going?'

The Negro straightened. He looked down at him. He looked at the twig in the tightly laced boot lying limp out and he remembered how the bwana's trail had been halting. The white man had picked on a strange vengeance. If he had meant to hunt out and kill Nebu, he should have gone unencumbered into the bush. But perhaps the bwana had been jiggling in the head all the while, not only today when he had been made beautiful. The night of the storm when he had strangled the msabu he had plainly been mad. If the animals had not finally got to him, burdened as he had been he would have perished from fatigue. But perhaps, when he felt that danger coming on, he would have rid himself of the boy. That was it. The bwana had known that the grey boy was not of his flesh and he would in the end have killed the toto. Working it out in his savage unsparing logic, Nebu came to that conclusion. The boy had been doomed from the beginning.

General Koko, who had lived in the white man's cities, had explained to them that the doctrine of brotherly love which the white man preached from his god was like the wings of the ostrich. No ostrich had ever flown by its wings.

'Hear me, brothers,' Koko said one day under the mimosa tree. 'Hear me. The white man builds houses of death in every one of his cities. In some there is a house for hangings, in others for beheading with a machine or an axe. In some they put their brothers into a chair to sit and then they send the electrical current through the chair and burn them to death. If they do that to their own white brothers, what will they not do to us?'

The boy laughed; peculiarly.

Nebu peered through the rain. 'Did you – laugh?'

'You will have to carry me, you know,' the boy said pleasantly.

Nebu shook his head slowly, thinking out the laughter.

'When he groaned and stumbled under me on the bad trails, my father called me a legacy which he would soon be happy to lose. My father was not very fond of me. Sometimes I think he was afraid of me. In Nairobi, when I laughed and told him that the other children called me the Grey Rat, he put his fingers over his eyes and peered through them at me. They said he was mad because the natives killed my mother the night I was born but he managed to save me. Why do you think he saved me first?'

The rain had got inside his head and Nebu heard it roaring between his ears. The thin grey face looked out at him from the tented covering of the sheet, a smile curving the soft lips; the brown doors were swinging wildly. Nebu caught glimpses, but he was not functioning.

'I was only an infant. I would not have felt anything. Why do you suppose he saved me?'

But the boy watched the Kikuyu stalk into the forest. And when he returned, his head bowed and face turned aside to avoid the long silver whips of rain elongating out of the sky, he bore a pair of stout staffs cut with a crook at the ends. He held them up before the boy and walked them forward in pantomime and then let them fall to the ground in front of him. Then he picked up the plastic folding cup which the boy had knocked from his hands, folded it down and put it into a pocket of the pea-jacket.

His grey face rigid, the boy took a long look at the crutches. He rose with the aid of the lean-to, the toe of the crippled foot trailing, and he tried the crutches and found they were no worse than those he had used in Nairobi or during the early part of the safari before he had dropped them in the river where the crocodiles showed their snouts, with glancing hope that his father would go in after them. He smiled at the black and followed him out of the camp.

11

In the town of Kiambu, in the concrete police post outside the cage of steel wire which was alive with black prisoners, the Inspector of Police agreed with the views of the army lieutenant who had just come in convoy from Nairobi. He agreed that such a campaign could fold this band of Kikes in a fist. The hard-mouthed young lieutenant swivelled the chair and leaned back, now that his views were home.

'All we need is a competent guide into that part of the country,' he said and looked the question.

'Gibson would be the man for it,' the inspector said.

'Then let's get him.'

'But Gibson has disappeared.'

'Disappeared? Who is he?'

'A planter. Funny business. Happened a fortnight ago. He and a crippled boy – son – of his.'

'You mean the blacks got him? Hasn't been reported, has it?'

The police officer shook his head. 'No. That is, we don't *know* it was Kikes. He just – vanished, he and the queer boy.'

'Then it's the Kikes all right. Queer? What do you mean, queer? Crippled?'

'Not that, no – well, he's just *queer*. But it's a long story – and a long-ago one. Happened before the Emergency, before my time, actually. His wife was killed at the time of the boy's birth. House burnt too. Could have been the first Mau Mau killing in these parts. Generally conceded it sent Gibson off his rocker. We never had it really sorted out. The black who was suspect disappeared about the same time, I am told.'

'Hmm. Anyway that won't help the price of fish. This guide, now. The niggers will not be expecting us now that their "long rains" have begun. We could knock them down with twenty to thirty men and a couple of mortars if we can move swiftly and surely through the infernal bush. Specially the bunch led by – what d'you call him?'

'Koko,' the policeman said. 'General Koko. I suppose we will be able to round up a good guide for you. Trouble is now that they think the Emergency is over they all want to do nothing else but plant coffee.'

The army man rose. 'Coffee? Remind them of the Lomans.' Tall and wide, he was brutal as a castle.

12

The rain clawed and kicked, shrieked and roared on the roof of the forest. It lashed at the tree-tops and came sullenly down the trunks with angry fluxions of its glistening coat. Branches broke beneath its weight, and it scoured out gullies among the roots. The storm had eaten the daylight; and in the dark the water-soaked trees gleamed like knuckles.

Nebu sloshed along in front, massive and shining in the rain-slick rubber. The boy hobbled behind him. The boy walked with his head down because the crutches sank in the soft spots and it tired him to fight them out of the mud. The crooked foot was a loose piece dangling a bit behind him. But his eyes were bright under the film of rain as they lifted at intervals to the heels of the man in front. The boy did not want to lose Nebu.

Nebu spoke to the beetle in his side. The beetle itched around under his skin, scratchy as a leopard on a tin roof. The bwana's bullet had been powerful. Even if it had not stayed in you, because your magic had been too strong for it, it was powerful enough to leave a beetle under your skin to remind you that it had called. The rifle at his back made him uneasy. He had slung it on out of pretension. He had not wanted the half-bwana to know how scared of it he was. But cold and dead as it was on his back, there was no telling what mischief it could be up to. It possessed some powerful magic.

A thought like a piece of wire slipped inside the boy's head. Back there in the camp, the nigger had bent down to look into his eyes and he did not all the while trust his eyes. One time, on the in-trail, '

Gibson had surprised the look in his eyes and had never after tha left him alone with the gun. Look, now. Notice this morning, when he had gone down stream to find a crap-house, he had taken the gun with him. But a fat lot of good it had done him. The thought slipped inside his head that just as the black had tried to read his eyes, he would read Nebu's mind through the soles of his feet.

Look at his big heels, like blobs of dirty suet pudding lifting and falling in the mud. I wonder what the nigger knows. The sole of his foot goes down into the bowels of the earth and comes up streaked with the dark secrets he carries in his nigger head. But the rain washes it clean before I can read it. The sole of his foot has eyes too. See how it evades the little islands of leaves and sticks? It knows that adders may lurk among the leaves.

He knew thorns which, if a man stepped on them, would send the poison leaping upward. Upward, until it closed about his heart. But he had no such hope. The black knew each inch of the land as a lion cub knew the tits. His – father, had worn boots up to his knees. He was right to still think of Gibson as his father. He was his father. The mad old fool had been lying when he had said that this—

He drew a big breath down into his narrow chest and felt big. Sometimes he wondered if it was wrong to be so big. Other people were content to be small and silly. Perhaps it was nicer to be small and silly. It was not always fun to know that with one sweep of your best thoughts to the front of your head you could kill one of the small sillies. He had fought more than once against the idea of killing Gib – his father and had succeeded in returning it to its place in the back of his head. There were also moments of weakness, when he was overcome with terror that the day would come when he was not able to push it to the back of his head; then he would be alone in the bush. But at that time the little goat-men of the moon would hold their sides and shriek laughter at him, winking that there would be room for him up there; he would not be left alone in any old bush. But he would have to fight hard to keep his

est thoughts from the front of his head every time he looked at the
lack.

*

The rain whanged with enthusiasm into the open places, glad to
meet the earth without having to fight a way past the trees. The
orrents here descended uncontested on Nebu's head and rolled off
he smooth mask face down his chest and gathered at his belt,
oaking down cold on his genitals. He pushed out his lower lip and
ulped in mouthfuls of the sweet water. It was water with gifts of
ure upper air, flowing straight from the hands of the Great Spirit.
t had abundant life, giving the tints to the lovely podo and making
he lilies sing. The sun-bleached red soil had turned dark, and often
lack, about. Later it would be fruitful, blooming in grass to feed
he gazelles who would please the lions.
   It had taken him not quite two days to get up to the bwana; but
hen he had been going flat out, running hard and full of spring at
is knees and ankles, sound in wind, no hole at his side to be careful
bout. And, at that time, he had been big with certainty that an
nemy had entered his country and had been delivered into his
ands. Now doubts wriggled in his mind. For the bwana had not
een a true enemy. Bwana Gibson had really been the wronged one.
Nebu marched old and hurt, looking for a cave.

*

Night, the true night, not the night of the rain and the trees,
cked tongues into all the corners, and licked darkest at the mouth
f the cave which Nebu had chosen for their shelter. It was bone-
ry from just within the door. It went in far into the cliff-face. The
lack stood well back and loosed three arrows into it and heard
hem *spang* at the back. No animal came hurtling out. He gathered
ticks inside the doorway and took the white man's petrol lighter
rom the pack and struck a fire. No snakes. So he went in and

45

recovered his arrows; one had the head broken off. He built up the fire and took off the wet rubber. The boy had already sunk down, the crutches propped against the wall. Nebu motioned at the pack, and the boy, after a speculative look, worked at the knots. He did not look back at the African again.

The fire burnt a great eye at the mouth of the cave. The black went out into the night and returned with pieces of dead wood which he stacked for the all-night fire. He caught rainwater into the pot and stood it on three stones at a corner of the fire. Coffee was in a large brown tin, a slab of bacon was wrapped in grease-proof paper. There were tins of flour and sugar and several of corned beef and sardines. He had never been so rich. When the coffee boiled, Nebu took Gibson's cup and held it out. The boy took up the pot and poured steadily.

The boy had shrill music he was listening to. It was louder than the rough swish of water through the trees, secret and splendid. This music never ran up and down like the music the Others tuned in on their wireless sets, but only ran in and out. This music came from the summit. Planetary stuff. It gave him the most wonderful ideas. One time, on the in-trail, when his father had taken him piggy-back through the bush, he had heard the music. After that, his father used to tie his hands when he took him piggy-back.

'I like camping at night,' he said while the black waited wordlessly for him to fill the cup. 'The children in Nairobi say I am like the gecko lizard. You know the gecko lizard? The ones with the grey skins who croak at nights? The children in Nairobi say I am like that lizard, and I used to croak for them and unskin my eyes. You want me to unskin my eyes? To croak for you?'

He held the pot away and worked his childish mouth into the hideous pucker of the gecko and gave the *urk urk urker urk*, his eyes bright on Nebu.

'And would you like to hear me laugh like the hyena? Or bark like the bull alligator?'

Nebu stared into the fire, hurt and bewildered. The payment he was making was not enough. For although the law only said that it should be flesh, the law also meant that it should be flesh you would be sad at, or made poorer by, losing. Like your fat cattle or she-goat, or the supreme one of a wife of great comfort. Not even the punishment was enough for what he had done to the bwana; for the hole in his side contained only a beetle. In some wounds a lion roared, or a leopard clawed itself; and in the death-wounds whole herds of elephants uprooted within. The half-bwana was a thin coin. Making recompense through such a boy would be cheating his way out of a debt. A son from the Masai girl would have been ample payment. She had limbs that made her sweet-moving as a slow river, a proud river. She broke like a queen, and at that time you knew that a son of hers would be coin from the mint, firm, unhandled.

Nebu sucked in a great gulp of the washed air drifting into the cave. He looked at the cocky grey animal who was slyly regarding him from the other side of the fire. Nebu knew the boy had been mocking him. He ducked a toe at the pack on the ground.

'Do you read the bwanas' God-book?' he asked softly.

The brown doors flashed open. 'You mean the Bible?'

Nebu remembered the old chief in the Adult Class. Redoubtable at debate in the tribal councils, the old man had plodded through the English books until he was invincible on the bwanas' own ground. He used the words he had heard the old chief use to a European policeman.

'Where-fore,' Nebu said awkwardly, 'let him that think-eth he stand-eth take heed lest he fall. First Co-rin-thi-an ten twelve.'

The boy clapped his hands and it echoed far back in the cave.

'Bravo!' he cried, hearing the music very shrill and loud.

Nebu grunted and ran his finger lightly around the ruffle of the wound's mouth, inside which the beetle was kicking up an itch.

13

The rain smashed on the stoop of the cave and exploded into spray. Moths died valiantly in it, struggling towards the fire brightly burning in the cave. Nebu, a blue-black god squatting quiet beyond comprehension, watched the Pink-wings and the House-builders and the Long-horns and all the little ones hurrying so devotedly into the fire. One alighted on the barrel of the rifle and folded its wings. It was fat, and pollen lifted from it into the air currents. *A weakling*, leaped the thought into Nebu's head. *Without spirit. Afraid to die.* He watched the unflinching ones enter the flame.

He took up the rifle and shook off the fearful one. The boy's head snatched out of the air and whipped around to watch him. Nebu put the barrel to his cheek and jerked on the moth's erratic course. The moth settled on the boy's forehead and Nebu snapped the rifle into position and pulled the trigger. 'Bang,' he said gravely. Angrily the boy slapped his forehead and squashed the moth.

'I killed him,' Nebu said. 'The weakling is dead.'

The boy looked into the mouth of the gun and the grey face whitened and the nostrils were pinched.

'You are in a mess,' he said thinly at Nebu. 'You are one Kikuyu in a mess. The white soldiers will kill you presently.'

'The insect is dead,' Nebu repeated. 'You saw me kill him?'

Those brown doors slipped open in the boy's eyes and the black leaned forward carefully looking for signs.

'You will never kill even a wish with that rifle!' he cried, shrill with it. 'My father was better than you, any day! Any time! He filled his pot and brought in any number of trophies too! See – he was a white man! You understand, nigger? He was a white man – that rifle is spooked for you, Kike!'

Nebu had it well stoked down. Soft was his voice, stroking towards the boy. 'The worms know no colour. And they stay underground when the long rains descend. But they will be occupied. Tomorrow the bwana will be without skin. The Great Father will not know him from me.' He had spoken in Kikuyu and now he was musing, hunched down with old truths as a prophet.

'That is the way of the Great One. We stand before him without skins. None is black, or white either. It is a mystery.'

'You are carrion!' the boy cried in that tongue.

And Nebu jerked under it, from head to toe. Then he recovered and looked away for as long a time as you could count up to twenty. But once again he looked at the boy.

'You speak my tongue,' he said in Kikuyu, solemn as bread. 'I am made happy to know that you speak my tongue.'

The boy made the same little formal bow which Nebu had given him and it was like at a tea. But he was all raw wires and sufferings inside. Nebu opened the jacket and scratched around with a finger and the boy saw there was a mouth to the wound.

'I would open that wound if I were you,' he said compassionately to the black, 'and let out some of that pus.'

He had the Negro staring blankly at him. 'The – pus?'

The boy took himself in hand and drew a seraph's face out of his grey, drawn looks. 'The bad water,' he said graciously. 'The pus. The water that kills.'

'It is a weak wound,' Nebu replied after a while. 'A beetle.' His finger went with husbanded energy around the itching wound.

The boy chortled amusedly in his belly. He was a one. Why did he think the black would allow him to open the wound? Why did he think the black trusted him? When he grew older he would use a knife. It must be a noble feeling to use a knife slowly and skilfully, watching the victim's face all the time. He had done it once on the setter bitch owned by the red bull of a man who had been his father, but his father had nearly killed him for it. And anyway, the face cut from lumber had never showed a thing; only opened its mouth and yelped something bitchy. The black's face would have shown it. All that goddam smooth skin would have crackled like stiff tissue gripped in your fist.

'You go to the white man's school?' Nebu asked suddenly.

The boy grinned. Really, would he quote scripture again?

'I go to the white man's school,' he agreed.

'And to his church?'

'And to his church.'

'And eat at table with them?'

Face full of childish malice: 'And eat with them, General Nebu. Do you?'

'And play with his totos?' the black asked eagerly. 'His children?'

The high music was singing in the boy, singing tall as a needle in his brain. He listened keenly to it and marched his fine, strong legs unstumblingly after the tuneful guidons, in and out among the booming, echoing stars. He was at home in the high, rushing light-roads and he knew them as he knew his numerals. Eleven plus thirty-one equals forty-two multiplied by thirteen equals five forty-six divided by seventeen equals thirty-two point one one eight to the nearest decimal. He was at the foot of the Second but he could do the maths the boys did in the Fourth Standard in his school. What did this addled nigger think? He hugged his thin chest in his arms.

'It is I who will not play with them, you black fool!' he shrieked at Nebu.

Nebu poked more wood into the fire and took the edge off the chill in the cave. The boy spoke Kikuyu and yet was one with the bwanas. It helped that he was proud too. When you stole from a man's house, the good recompense was to return the value of the goods you had stolen, or better. The bad requital was to return something less in value. The sick little half-bwana had acquired more value by speaking the Kikuyu tongue. He would take more of Nebu with him when he returned into the white man's camp. Perhaps as they journeyed through the bush something more of value would turn up. Nebu spoke affectionately to the Great One about the fleck of sunlight which had fallen on him, and took up the rifle again. But the Great One smote his knuckles and his fingers slipped from the rifle. He nodded. He clearly understood.

He should not be pushing. It would be ascertained in his head when the Great One was satisfied.

He drew the rifle beside him and rolled himself in the blanket and lay down, feet towards the fire. The beetle was active in his side. This pain, too, was recompense. It was the law.

14

In the night the wood was eaten wider and the fire shrank, and the boy lay awake listening to the rain. The shadows in the cave over-powered the light and squeezed it to a slit around the embers. Outside, the savagely hungry floods tore away and swallowed chunks of earth big enough for an earthquake to eat. Great boulders crashed like siege guns.

It was like telling lies in the Confessional. That was it. Bad as telling lies in the Confessional – not to have made something happen to the silly black long ago. One could have understood his failure where his father was concerned. Tying his hands every night was no joke. But he had turned it neatly – going to his knees each night in the boma, the fingers interlaced above corded hands, and his face made into a seraphim just as those on the walls of the church in Nairobi. And then putting down the massive corner-stone of the Our Father and strewing the seven graceful Hail Marys round and round it ... *Blessed art thou amongst women and blessed is the fruit of thy womb, Jesus* ... and how the Red Bull used to squirm! *Pray for us sinners, now*, looking full-eyed into his father's face. But the Red Bull had not been ninnied, ever. The hands had remained tied together. And now, here he was, free.

He turned his head to shoot a glance at the black. Slumber had collected Nebu into the blanket, tight as a sausage.

Nebu slept like his land, the unlooted portion of the forests and rivers. His eyes were closed and only the gentle heaving of the blanket showed that life was thereabout. His sleep was in rhythm with the land, and if the rain had ceased or the wind had died, he

52

would have instantly waked. As he did just now when the continent tilted towards the sun.

He slipped out of sleep as he had slipped into it, a brush of a feather, but an aura from the boy collided with it and the warning made the grey face work insanely as the boy sank back into his bed. The black's eyes quickly roved the cave and ran to the door, where the dark flood descended. There was no light there but Nebu had heard the dawn coming. A lizard, wet and shivering under a leaf, had croaked of it. A big cat, nervous of the water, had coughed it. He sat up and put wood into the fire and the shadows leaped away.

The wound had grown a beard in the night. It was older, had grown a beard and was clawing its boots for balance among his entrails. Pain foamed in his bowels. When the Masai men in the bush grew past forty, the hard young tribesmen walked away from them and they were left to their old woman and the lions. Then they built a boma near a stream and blocked dung into bricks and built a hut and waited in the boma to die. You came upon them sometimes, hawk-eyes dusty, veined, their bones proud at knees and elbows, their bellies like footballs gurgling with wind. And they held their spears not like sunbeams straying through their fingers but like butchers' hatchets in the meat market. They tethered their cattle and threw away their bullwhips.

*

As he remembered the great illumination of the moon at the ngoma when he was made a morani, a young warrior, so he remembered his first going with Koko and what the bullwhips did. They caught the white Special Constable on the road outside the market and knocked him on the head and took him into the bush. That was the time of the Strange Feeling.

'Look at him, all of you!' cried Koko at the new ones, touching the bright yellow khaki of the young settler with his stick. 'Look at him and undergo the strange feeling.'

And the white constable had folded himself into a bright yellow ball in the mud and looked up at them in terror.

'Bow down to us, to Africa – you unlikeliness!' screamed Koko at him. 'Free my young men of the strange feeling – teach them how to stand while the bwanas kneel in the mud!'

And he signalled by a snap of his fingers to the young men with the bullwhips, who slowly tore the flesh from the policeman. They tore his clothes first, the buffalo-hide whips cutting through cake. Marvellously, they undressed him, a baby in a tub, while he squirmed and wept and shrieked in the filth. And the moranis who had been magnificent cattle-boys before the Emergency spilt not a drop of blood until he was divested, and even then the blood came in pin-pricks, in precious rubies.

*

The Negro stretched his cramped legs nearer the fire and the wound clamoured at his side. He drew down the blanket and lifted the end of the jacket and saw the gay flush of poison in his flesh. It had swollen fist-sized in the night. He warmed his hands at the fire and pressed them around the mouth of the wound. The agony made his teeth slip sideways. He stepped out of the blanket and went to the door of the cave. He gathered wet clay and made a fresh poultice. The pain spurted under his fingers. He looked up and the day looked back at him from slitted eyes at the top of the trees. He returned to the fire.

The boy sat up and said: 'Just listen to that rain.'

Nebu stirred the soup he had poured into the pot from a paper packet.

'My father said that in England, on a day like this, someone would come along and say: "It's a fine day." '

Nebu put down the spoon and looked at the boy. He said in Kikuyu: 'Fine days happen in the heart, toto.'

The boy laughed and switched to Kikuyu. 'You must have been a priest in your village before you turned bandit.'

'All priests are bandits and all bandits are priests. All chiefs are beggars and all beggars are chiefs. Men are what they are when they are.'

The boy's eyes shone. He spoke merrily. 'It's good to know you feel like talking. Is it because we are speaking Kike? Or are you like this only on rainy days? My father said the niggers went crazy on the nights of full moon, or at the commencement of the long rains. Is it true, General Nebu? Do *you* run amuck in the long rains?'

It went past Nebu and disappeared through the mouth of the cave. A bubble rose in his head and he pricked it with the thought that the toto might have eaten a pie of parrot. The toto could not know what had happened.

'Golly, I would like to see you run amuck,' the boy said, an engaging grin on the thin grey face. He rocked back on his buttocks and gripped the crippled foot like a satchel under his arm.

Nebu finished the broth and took it from the fire and poured it into two bowls. He handed one to the boy.

'Eat, toto of the long tongue. We go far today.'

The grin slipped mockingly down the boy's face. It raised itself when he put the bowl to his mouth and it looked at Nebu over the edge. But Nebu ate and walked his mind over the trail ahead today. The rivers would be fat and murderous now that they were strengthened by the rain. He would go the long way, circling the rougher rivers. He was growing a garden at his side. He could feel the flowers growing, gay, poison flowers. He felt the mocking slice of the boy's eyes carve criss-cross over his face. He gave no sign that he felt it.

'What do you expect to gain from me?' the boy asked suddenly. He was holding the bowl waist-high, gazing at Nebu. 'Ransom? Like in the books?'

The word for *ransom* is the same as for *loot* in Kikuyu and the laughter at it left Nebu's head, stepped a yard out and looked at him, and jumped back in again.

'I have nobody, you know. Nobody at all,' the boy said sadly. 'You killed the only one I had.'

'Eat,' the black said harshly.

The boy's fingers opened and the bowl fell, spattering and causing some hissing disturbances at the edge of the fire. Seated on the horn of the moon, he looked down at Nebu.

'Your voice was like my father's,' the boy said up there.

Nebu picked up the fallen bowl and put it telescope-fashion into his own. He handed them to the boy. He took the ends of the four-in-hand ropes on the pack and spread them on the floor and threw in the foreign treasures: the pairs of socks cruelly balled, the clean but limply folded shirts and undergarments, the crafty razor hiding in its case.

The bwana could have killed me instead, Nebu said to himself as he worked. *So what is death? Death is to be slow for life. It is to have been slow in dodging the arrow or the sleeping sickness or the falling tree. Yet a man cannot fail to be slow, at some time. It is the law.*

He worked at the thought solemnly, wonderingly, as at a poem. *Sometimes the wind flees ahead of the rain and then it slows for a mountain and is touched by the swordsmen. But does the wind die? The wind is not dead. It has gone into the rain. Oh, now the rain is cavalry of the royal household, pennants flying, silver hooves hitting, and the old bent earth slips backward, backward, curved at the spine, cowering.*

He said, slapping the soft leather of the bwana's mosquito boots: 'When Nebu dies, a part of him will enter Koko, or, maybe, someone else, to make him stronger. A man is never sure. Just as he is unsure to whom will ultimately go that portion of himself when he tires and dies on top of a woman.'

He rubbed the soft leather. He felt it coming. 'Life is like the wind, blowing equally, first from the east and then from the west. It withers, but never dies.' And at last the white imagery strutted loudly forth: 'Like the endless strings of sausages hung in the great stores of Nairobi, all their withered ends meeting to puff flatly again.'

'Lord love a duck!' the boy whispered in English.

Nebu finished the knot. He spoke to the boy the formal words which opened a journey: 'Let us look around the corner, toto.'

15

'It is the wound,' the boy said softly, swinging like a question mark on the crutch as he halted and looked carefully at Nebu's face when the black stopped. 'It has the poison in it.'

Since they had started, the wound had glowed dully at his side; but just now he had slipped and the wound had burst into light, shedding pain in him. He held it and sweated. Nebu listened to the agony talking in him and waited for it to be silent. He wrote it in his head that the toto had a false face.

The day dragged itself down through the trees, pale, sickly, the sun had no blood for it. The wind was axing the underbrush. The rain had eased but Nebu knew it would strike down again, for it was so the long rains fell. For a time it would hector as a shrill wife and then grow tender as it now was. But when you bared your head to it and held out your hands for it to anoint, suddenly it drove down again, brutally, tearing your faith into shreds. Life sometimes fooled you as adroitly as the rain; like the lakes down on the plains whose placid lovely surfaces were roofs to bull alligators.

Now the pain was falling soft as pine needles and Nebu went on ahead of the boy. Far off, the rain sounded. They were crossing a neck of tall grass and in it was an island of bamboos, aloof as cats. He chopped down his hand for the boy to stand where he was and he crossed to the bamboo stand. He swung the panga at some tall shoots. He shredded the shoots of spiny branches as he returned and when they had got inside the tree-line he stopped and split them straight down and cut them into foot-long lengths. He found lianas and plaited some mattings. He thonged a pair to his own feet and fixed one to the healthy foot of the boy and the others to the ends of the crutches. The boy tried it and he was solid in the mud as a pillar.

'You are very clever for a black,' the boy said in English and repeated it in Kikuyu using the word *Kikuyu* for *black*.

The rain sounded again and caught up with them and the trees bent over their heads and acted as leaky umbrellas. But they had the ground-sheets up and the water poured down them, coming in only at their ankles.

'Some Kikuyus are clever and some are stupid,' Nebu said in his tongue. 'Some white men are clever and some are stupid. Are you a clever white boy or a stupid one?'

The boy spoke under his breath. Nebu unslung the rifle and turned it about in his hand. All of it, as he had seen in Koko's, was there: the oiled barrel which shed water like a duck's back, the unspeakably lewd mouth, the sober trigger. And Nebu made game at himself that although his rifle was the twin of Koko's, this twin brother was a man of quiet deeds and shrank from all public outcry. If he pointed this brother at that gnarled old wild olive and waited long enough, it would kill whatever animal that was which was occupying the lowest limb. Then as he drew nearer to the olive and identified the dark brown, wet, carpety abandon on the limb, Nebu sucked in his breath. The rifle dropped at his feet as his hands threw into motion. The heavy iron spear fell into his hand, balanced between thumb and fingers. One leg bent and forward, Nebu waited for the leopard's spring, and beyond the strangeness of awaiting the charge of a cat in a rain-shrouded forest was the knowledge like an angering, disturbing blow that the leopard was in front of him, waiting for him.

The big head swung, the yellow-green unblinking eyes met his for an instant before the beast left the limb in a single bound that hid it in the undergrowth. And knowledge further sprouted in Nebu that he was being stalked.

16

Nebu found a cave before dark and he stacked in sufficient wood to keep the fire in good spirits until daylight. He built a pyramid of stones at the entrance, sealing it to animals, and then he looked at the wound and smelled pus. Towards morning, the smell came to him again and the pain with it. He stayed with it, knowing it to be bad, but unable to think of anything more useful than wet clay. In the village, the old women would have chewed herbs to poultice the wound and he would have healed. Out here he was a man past forty and left for the lions – or the leopard somewhere outside in the half-dark eyeing the fire and considering all sorts of brave thoughts except that of crossing the fire-line. No leopard would cross the fire-line. He would wait until you grew big with carelessness and passed beneath his limb, and then leap for your back and sink his teeth into the place where your neck and shoulder joined; stuck like a brown burr on a cabbage. He remembered a leopard he had seen loping through the bush with a buck in its mouth. The buck was still alive and the eyes were blank with terror. And the leopard had watched the black from the corner of its eyes, a warning growl bristling out of the sides of its mouth; like a wreath-of-thorn design around the bone-stiff buck.

Nebu, wrapped in the blanket and lying by the fire, remembered the whole globe of subjects, but he could not forget the smell of pus.

The boy lay awake thinking of the time when he had caught the mouse and locked it in the room with the house cat while he watched through a window, and the way the mouse had gone up, rearing, a tank on hind-legs, but unable to obstruct the god-cat when it smote in. The back broke, and the boy shivered deliciously remembering the deflated buttocks and the limp tail when it dragged its ruins in circles before it was speared for the meal. He remembered when the cat was finished how he had gone into the room and picked it up and turned up the paw and stared in fascination at the killer thing now sheathed and innocuous. And he rose to his elbow when the black turned uneasily and he called softly across the cave:

'Good morning, Nebu. It is another lovely day, isn't it?'
Feeling very good. Uplifted. In a state of grace.

PART TWO

17

The leopard came out in the afternoon. It came out of a clump of husky chestnuts, off a low limb, and it was cold and wet and murderous. Save for the quick scrabble of the claws on the slippery wood, it left the limb without a sound; and when Nebu saw it the hind-legs were already hooking inward for sinking into the boy's shoulders. It was an alien flicker in the corner of Nebu's eyes but his jungle senses instantly smote into action. He was quicker than the cat, with the upward lunge of the spear. But the flying brute curved magnificently in the air, striking at the iron as it passed. Nebu felt the earthquake in his shoulder, in his arm, as the point raked savagely, helplessly, along the turning, cheating hard-skinned coat.

It dropped squarely and the fore-legs hit and bounded off the turf like rubber pads. Snarling, it pivoted on hind-legs. The great head slashed around and Nebu looked full into the face of the cat. Hate, fury, purpose, flourished like green things in the tawny face; desiring Nebu, rippling to tear him down. The claws drew red wounds into the earth. The claws were dirty, Nebu noticed. The boy whimpered where he had fallen to the ground and the sound drew the reptilian head around to him and the pouched lips lifted off the teeth.

'No!' Nebu cried.

Anything to turn the pouring eyes back to himself.

He gestured with the seven-foot spear.

'No! Child of filth! To me! Me! Carrion! Work for your meal!'

Like the nobler ones of the forest. And Nebu heard the animal purr and he saw how the end of the tail moved lightly, and his bowels contracted as under a sharp blow and he lurched forward, yelling.

He would have plunged the spear into it but the leopard groped in the ground and found footing, hurled itself backward and was gone with two bounds into the bush. Nebu waited until the crash of its going was lost to the clearing.

He turned his head up to the rain. The insolent rain splashed on his forehead and ran down into his mouth. He blinked it out of his eyes. He looked down, clear-eyed, at the boy and he broke at the middle. The boy was very still, very wide-eyed now, staring to where the leopard had vanished. The pain leaped into the African's side and he felt it go down into his legs, moving liquidly, filling him with a great warm hurt: majesty, agonized.

'It is you who smell of death,' he said, tall again above the boy.

The grey face tilted a worried look up at him.

'Why do you say that? Why?'

Urgent.

'The leopard spoke, young bwana,' Nebu told him. 'He said he had come for you.'

'Don't be a fool!' cried the boy, scrambling upright and gathering the crutches. 'You are nothing more than a superstitious black!'

One of the mattings had dropped from the crutches and Nebu went down and re-fastened it. There was majesty in this also.

'Why didn't you kill him? Is he one of your native gods too?'

Jeering.

As the half-bwana had said, he should have killed the leopard. He should have thrown the spear, the cat had been less than a buck's jump away. But the body with which he was so intimate had spoken in the clearest tones of the weakness in it. One did not hurl a death-throw with the heart alone. One collected the blood and sinews and skill into a single sublime moment and threw with finality. He had felt the fault in his body when he had drawn back his arm, the fault that had been placed there by Bwana Gibson's bullet. He might have wounded the beast. But a whelping she-lion was a new-born lamb compared with a wounded leopard.

'I should have used the white man's gun to protect his toto,' Nebu said. 'Then the white man's god would have relented and made the gun speak for the white man's son.'

The boy's eyes drove daggers into the back of the black's bowed head, for he thought he had heard mockery in the Negro's voice. His hip was smarting, where he had hit the ground when fright threw him, but he had seen the leopard before Nebu had. He had even seen it just before it left the branch, for he had been a little behind and to one side of Nebu. But it had not occurred to him that the cat had been after *him*. And it had been, afterwards, the oddest feeling, watching the stinking, muscular arms opening to embrace him, to see the claws coming out of their sheaths, slow as a girl's grin while she wondered whether to hurt you. The black had been quick, he could say that about him. But to be now mocking him! Unthinkable. The injury paraded kingly through him as he glared down on the curly nigger-head fastening the silly things to the crutches.

He said, when Nebu straightened: 'The rifle is useless to you. Stick to your primitive weapons: your bow and arrows. What about your bow and arrows? Why didn't you use this big bow?'

'One does not walk the forest with a loaded bow.'

'The white man walks the forest with a loaded gun. The black walks the forest with an empty bow,' the boy said understandingly.

'And so there are accidents,' Nebu joked, still-faced as a stone. 'Has the young bwana ever heard of a black man killed accidentally by a bow? Or a spear? These are made for Africa.'

'Yet the white man's guns kill your spearmen!' the boy cried furiously.

'Numberlessly,' Nebu said quietly.

He stalked forward, holding the pain in him and thinking how it was like the hourglass outside the Bwana Gibson's house. When it was drained out, you turned it about and it was born again. The pain should drain from his body and leave him clean of sand as was the upper half of the glass: to make his blood flow pure again, the muscles quick, eyes clear, to make him cope with the bush and the strange toto who walked with him. Tomorrow he hoped to be up at the sulphur pool, the place of big healing.

*

The rain lashed with more violence and the wind bustled the large trees and bent the saplings double. He adjusted the rubber sheeting over his head and watched the grey old face of the boy peer anxiously out of his cape at the dark, whirling world. In the yellow-shot dark of the rainstorm, Nebu saw the erect pink flowers of chestnuts and the laburnums beaten into the mud, and the leaves of the wild figs thick and deformed under the water pouring from them; and he wondered, as he had always wondered when he was a child, where did the lions and the buffaloes and rhinos cower in the storm? And where did the elands and the gazelles gallop to, when the floods opened over their heads. And did the eagles and the heavenly flamingoes kill their pride and weep among the rocks when the long rains loosened?

Beyond the limits of the land where the tribe hunted, marked by those humpy hills rising and falling three days' journey to the east, the sun first thrust up the straight yellow shafts and you could see them swelling with growth, throbbing and widening as the golden ball hauled its weight up them, until, fat with fun, the great globe broke above the hills laughing wildly, and the night ran howling off the land.

They had lain with their heads outside the hut door watching the day come, and they had been young and unspent as the day, the final shards of glory swinging in their bellies, bars of music tinkling yet.

'I will hunt and fish and work in our garden,' he had said. 'And by the winter I will have earned the cattle and sheep for the dowry.'

'I will wait while my man does all these things,' the new-made woman said, 'and bear his children when he returns.'

'They will be great men, these children,' said the new-made husband.

'And faithful women,' she said.

'And mothers of other great men.'

'And other good women,' she said into the growing dawn.

'Were you – were you – not afraid last night?' asked the brave young man.

He shucked his body into position to see her face. He wondered at it. He wondered at the strength there and was awed that he had heard her whimper. And he wondered at the composed mouth and unruffled forehead and tender eyes and he felt safe with her, as if with her he would stand boldly out among lions, or in the street of a hostile village, or before all the guns of raiding white men.

'The – pain?' Needing to shake her, the old man-need. 'The pain?'

'It had already been taken from me by the knives of the magpie old women,' she said and they both laughed at the memories of the circumcision rites, and then were solemn at it too.

He said: 'Tomorrow I will commence to build our hut.'

'Tomorrow is today,' said the girl whom the tribe had chosen to be his wife. 'Today. Now, my lazy young husband.'

But the sweetness was stirring in his limbs once more and today they would be undisturbed in the nuptial hut.

'Did you – hope – it would be Nebu?' The pride never really absent from love.

And she wrote the answer in her eyes and laughed deeply and gloriously and wonderfully hurt at his sweet ignorance. She had climbed lovely hills in the Nakuru district and swum the lake at Naivasha and swung through the forests bearing mountainous baskets of potatoes and bado and moulded her body to be a princess fit for such a morning with Nebu. She would please him or disembowel herself. She would wash and cook for him, and carry his pots and spears, so long as she could love him carefully, competently, warmly, wantonly. But she would mystify him, storing her answers only in her eyes while her heart sang with the joy of it.

'A swallow flew in your eyes a while ago,' he said.

'No,' she said. 'It stood and sang for you.'

'For me?'

'For us, and our sons and daughters,' reading in the ignorant young man's eyes that it would be true. And she turned to lie out and look up at the strongly flushing sky through the trees and the birds flying. And her sweet limbs arranged themselves to be perfect and good for him, giving much and taking much, in rhythm with him.

18

'The evening is on us,' Nebu said next day to the doggedly plod-
ding boy whom he now made walk before him. 'Tomorrow, or the
day after, we should be on the white man's road.'

'That is if the leopard doesn't get to you first. You smell of pus,'
The boy retorted viciously.

'Pus? The bad water? That is the smell of life, young bwana.'

But he could smell it too and the pain was rampaging. He had
fought it all day, fought against a halt except for food. But his
mind was now made up. He would pause at the place of sulphur.
the clay had done the wound no good and he did not know the
right herbs. Bathing in the place of sulphur would slay the
elephants in his side. He had not seen the leopard all today but he
knew it was never far away. It would stalk upwind of them, prowling from branch to branch, taking to the ground when the trees
thinned out but keeping to the tall grass, pausing to scratch and
yawn, yellow eyes unwinking, ugly head swinging side to side,
alert for food or enemies.

'I – I suppose you will be taking me into some town or other,' the
boy said, cocking his ears for the reply.

'You will be safe when you are near to the white men,' Nebu
said.

'Not if you leave me on the road. There are wild beasts on the
road.'

'In the towns too,' Nebu said sharply.

The boy chuckled, getting it. 'Yes, the white men will tear you to
bits for treating a young bwana as you have treated me. Fact is, you

are nothing but a wild beast yourself. My father said all the blacks were wild beasts.'

'Who saved you yesterday?' Nebu retorted steadily, thinking that clack-clack goes the half-bwana's tongue only to bruise.

'The ransom,' the boy said, crooking his pale face in a grin up at Nebu. 'The nice fat ransom you hope the white men will pay you for the young bwana.'

The rain had let up, but the small trees showered when the wind shook them. The wind slipped, when it could, furtively out of the underbrush, bringing to Nebu the scents of his land, the slow sweet scents of the night-blooming jasmine and the mutoma and the musk odour of the soaked hollows which had been abandoned by the animals. But he ignored all these, thinking of the boy.

'I'll bet you are sorry you are a nigger.'

You would win, Nebu thought clearly. *You would win your bet because I am weakening and tired and I want the white man's magic to heal the great wound. No other reason.*

'Day after tomorrow you will be there,' he said steadily.

19

Fighting is a tiring thing, Nebu said to the Lawgiver early in the morning. *It blares like trumpets in the beginning and then it becomes a cracked cymbal. It has a stale taste when you cannot conquer.*

Nebu had heard it early in the morning. The big drum that was his heart, pounding hugely, and the rapid beats of the smaller drums at his wrists and forehead. They enveloped him, deafened him; and he had the rushes of hot piping pain more frequently now. He turned; and it turned with him. He sat up in the blankets and it rose with him, this close bedfellow. It was difficult to extend his legs, for the poison had drained heavily into them. His shoulders spoke to him, not strongly, but distinctly enough, that they were usefully with him; but the legs worried him.

The legs wondered to themselves whether the miles of mountain and plateaux stretching in front of them could be successfully plundered for the lord to whom they owed allegiance.

From his waist down, he had swollen badly in the night. But he was nearing the place of sulphur. He knew the landmarks and he was sure to bathe tomorrow.

The black braced himself off the floor of the cave and stood by the fire. The strong, indomitable neck flowing unceasingly wide into the arrogant head, hooded with the effort to stand. He swallowed saliva which tasted brittle. The cave was floored with pain when he walked to the opening. He looked outside and returned to the fire. He considered, standing.

But you may win – if you can die, Nebu said to the Lawgiver. The Lawgiver nodded, remote.

The boy was fitful, troubled, angry at the unknown. He felt quite capable with the black, but the leopard was a page he had not turned. He had not told this to the superstitious black, but he had distinctly heard the leopard call his name when he had fallen to the ground and the brute had whirled and looked at him. He did not know how the leopard could have got his name. Nobody within miles knew it. He had not even told it to the black. Then how could the filthy cat have known it? He wished there was something he could do to the leopard, but he had not been able to think of a thing all the night. He had merely floated aimlessly up there, listening to the music. He watched Nebu walk to the mouth of the cave. The stink of pus was all about the cave. He could safely write off that one. It was the leopard which bothered him now.

'I'll bet you have scared him off!' he cried, suddenly.

Nebu looked up from the fire and met the hard brightness in the boy's eyes.

'Good morning,' the Negro said. 'It is a lovely morning.'

The boy grinned and licked his lips. He could hear the roar of the early downpour. 'You remembered, General Nebu? That is what my father used to say. That is, I mean was, a pretty how–d'ye-do. You think he will be back today?'

'Who? Your father?'

The boy shot up angrily out of the blankets. 'You dam' black! You dare to joke with me! You know I meant the leopard which your clumsiness made escape us!'

Nebu said gravely: 'Speak to the rifle for me and then we need not fear Bwana Leopard's return.'

The boy sputtered lightning words. But soon he sat down on his anger and grinned mischievously and said: 'The spear is the black man's weapon. And the bow. Don't you want to use your own weapons? Are you ashamed of being a nigger?'

The bow, the wanderobo, was six foot tall, and he had cut the first from the heart of the m'pweki wood when he had returned from the bush where the elders had sent all the young men to be made, out of fortitude and fending for themselves, into warriors, into proud young morani. He could remember the day he had put away the bow and gone to work for the bwanas. This one, the wanderobo he now carried, he had made years later, after the time of the man-love, up near the snow-line.

He took it up while the water heated and took in the buffalo thong a few inches because it had been slackened by the damp. He fixed his fingers around the thong and tested the pull. He felt the pull at his waist and it shrieked all the way down his swollen legs and he released it to thwack harmlessly back. The sweat pushed out on his forehead. His wrists were long and flexible and very strong. He gazed numbly at them extended before him and thought of his legs. His legs had been long and thin and fitted into the flat belly with distinction. Now they were gross: fat, weak trees, like the Congo bean, blown up by air and water. A yard would be a mile. They belonged to the High Court judge in Nairobi. They were strangers.

'Not so good, is it?' the boy asked softly. 'You should have made me lance it. Bleed out the pus. I told you.'

A little sorrow, Nebu told his Kikuyu heart, *a little sadness, a stir of joy – a little of everything. That is life.*

And the Lawgiver nodded. He smiled inside. The water boiled.

Nebu lifted the pot from the edge of the fire and rested it on the floor. He dipped the end of cloth in it and raised the jacket to get at the wound. He shrank at the sight. The boy rose and hopped quickly to his side.

'Here,' the boy said, 'let me hold it.' He took the pot and held it close to the black.

Nebu pressed the hot cloth to the wound and the elephants in there uprooted trees. The great voices of pain whooped in Nebu, and in the midst of the clamour he exploded.

*

The Great One must have glued the agonized little pieces together, for he returned from absolute darkness into agonizing light. Groping forward out of the ruins, he felt the wetness on his feet and then he saw the overturned pot on the floor and the boy crouched in a corner of the cave staring at him.

'You moved suddenly!' the boy cried, seeing himself crucified in the black's eyes. 'It – it – slipped out of my hand!'

But in his head he was writing down how like lumber, a piece of ebony, the face of Nebu had been. Suffering unmoved just like the dog long ago. And he was furious at Nebu for not exposing the pain. What thrill was there if it was not exposed? The blacks were just like beasts.

The Negro stumbled forward out of the destruction and acknowledged the boy's words with a grunt. He sniffed and shook his head, coming out from under tons of fallen rock. Under his lowered brow, he watched the boy closely. He was sure he had caught a glimpse. He breathed in sadly at it. It was as well that the beetle had left the wound and that the elephants were trumpeting now. The recompense he was offering was not suitable. Not suitable at all.

'Yet the young bwana accused me of clumsiness,' he said gently. But there was nothing to be seen. The brown doors had swung shut. 'Let us eat, and go.'

Because of the inroads they had made into the stack of tins, the pack had been considerably lightened. Now Nebu left in the cave the foods they would not be needing for their journey to the road. He also left the wanderobo, taking only the panga and spear. The panga was thonged to his body, was a part of him for he slept with it there. The spear was no more obstruction than his arm. He could not pull the bow. He also took the rifle.

His speed was dictated by the boy's hobble, so at first he walked comfortably enough despite the swollen legs. But the boy's merry chuckle was not unexpected.

'I think it is funny, General Nebu. Really funny,' the boy said. 'Here we are, a pair of cripples. Two cripples. I'll bet the leopard

74

will not be able to make up his mind which of us to take first.'

Nebu said nothing, holding in his strength. He was guiding the boy by touching him on the right or left shoulder with the butt of the spear; touching him on the top of his head when he wanted a halt. He had his own solemn humour when he had the notion that the young half-bwana walking before him was a calf being driven to the market place to be haggled over, bargained with, the hock and liver bringing so much. He moved carefully along, keyed to swift action, in eyes and arms at least. The smell of pus was too strong to escape the leopard. Lower down the slope the hyena would join the leopard. But he had no fear of the hyena; as for a different reason he had no fear of the nobler animals who shunned decay. Without bothering to be sorry for himself, he knew he was decaying. The leopard grew more ferocious when he stalked the wounded or the weak. He gripped down hard on the iron in his hand. The song in his back and shoulders was comfortably near to the perfect tune he had known before the bwana's bullet struck him.

'Let us say to him when he comes,' the boy said gaily, 'let us say: "Mr Leopard, before you choose, think who will be the bigger meal. Think and choose well, Mr Leopard!"'

Nebu guided him to the right, out of the treeline, towards a patch of limestone gleaming in the dusky, rain-swept plateau.

'Half of you is rotting already while I am sound,' laughed the boy merrily. 'So, General Nebu, you will have to fight for *your* life.'

Nebu tapped him on the head and the boy halted. The black said: 'It is the place of sulphur.'

He pointed the spear to the steaming little pool in the basin of the limestone. 'I will bathe the great wound here while you stand and watch for the leopard.'

The plateau was covered with low grass and Nebu had no fear that the leopard would try to slip up to them. Leopards struck from ambush, from the low trees, or from the tall grass through which they made their famous golden rushes, the tawny coat blurred in speed to the colour of dirty gold. The negro carefully peeled away

75

the clothes from his swollen limbs and stepped into the pool. The bubbling water turned milky when his feet stirred the lime deposits. When he sat down the surface drew well above his hips, warmly, a mother of great love. It clothed and fed him and sheltered him. There was a wound throbbing, but it was pain happening in another house. He could see the fires burning across the street in the other house, and there were strangers watching around the sick one.

*

He had commenced the slow, hard gathering of the dowry the day after, gaining the cattle and the goats as payment for herding for his father during the cold winter nights; standing taut by his spear in the hot, short days, eyes caked and burning by reason of the unending watch for marauding cats. And one day towards the end of the year when the long rains ended and the plateau came alive with young grass-shoots friskily gambolling with the wind, he had herded the flock the fortnight's journey over hills and through long valleys to the ridge above the village. He had halted before the ridge.

Puzzled, young Nebu sniffed the smoke and listened. It came weakly up, floating bodilessly, the *dum-da-da-dum*, beaten with the back of the hand, the death drum.

And uncertain whether the village had been raided by the ferocious Somali, or had been punished by some punitive party from the white man's town, the youthful Nebu had crawled forward to the ridge and looked down. His village was dead. Hyenas slunk in and out.

The discredited witch-doctor, who had failed to stop the Kaffir pox and who had moreover fallen himself a victim to it and was dying over his drum, told him. What was left of the village had moved on, leaving the dead and dying. She had died early. The witch-doctor, fully clothed in the deadly lumps, beat the drum slowly with the back of his hand.

*

'The leopard!' the boy cried out. 'Nebu, the leopard!'

The body that the black burdensomely raised from the pool was heavy as an elephant's. He was an old woman, stepping from the pool. The warm water poured down his thighs, and the air, turned cold now, dug him with needles. The boy was swinging excitedly on a single crutch, flapping his hand towards the trees.

'He came out from there. I – I saw him creeping towards me and – and – I shouted and flung the crutch at him! Then he turned and bolted back among the trees!'

Nebu searched the trees with his eyes but saw no signs. It was the custom when they sought healing in the pool to soak from dawn to noon but the black remembered the sick, sour body he had with difficulty lifted out of the water and he knew he had slowed up too considerably for him to risk being in the water if the beast struck. Awkwardly, he dressed, picked up his weapons and motioned to the boy to go on. The boy looked helplessly at him.

'The crutch – I threw it at him. It fell behind the rock – there.'

Behind the rock where the clump of ferns flourished like a mass of green lace. He nodded, knowing what hard going the soggy ground was for the boy. He went over to retrieve it, stopped, and the mamba that had been curled among the ferns, struck. But the frightened serpent had moved too early and Nebu with a soft grunt flung away before it could coil to strike again. Then with a quick swing of the panga he sliced away the head.

The smooth black mask with the unseeing jewelled eyes turned to the boy and went past him and Nebu looked out at the hills, which seemed engraved in stiffened smoke. The question stirred slowly in his breast.

'Pick it up,' he said. A thousand years old he was. 'Pick it up, white boy.'

The boy's face was closed against the African. A queer dignity went with him as he moved forward on the stick and he didn't seem to hobble at all. He picked up the staff he had tossed into the ferns when he had seen the mamba slither there to hide. He shook off the beheaded thing and wiped the wood in the grass. He tucked the crutch under his arm and swung round, facing the Kikuyu

'There was no leopard,' Nebu said lonely, wearily, nobody in hi house.

The clean-limbed athlete who was the murderer in the boy ran lightly out of him and swung to the horn of the moon. Grinning happily, he dangled his sound legs and listened to shrill music. Rain dimpled the surface of the pool and Nebu drew the ground-sheet over his head and motioned the boy ahead. Protected under a fold of rock a mile down-wind, the leopard rose and yawned and slipped out to the wet again.

20

Nebu said to the long muscle that springs like a bow from kneecap to hip: *There are hills to cross today.*

His head was filled with the hills, light green hills and dark ones, hills where buttercups blazed like yellow fires at dusk; hills that were long-drawn-out shrieks on whose slopes the best would bucket; and the wrinkled, mean, nut-brown ones that would twist your ankle and your soul. Yet Nebu knew that save for the general upcurve of the valley he was in, upcurving to the kopje where the Nairobi road looped nearest towards him, there would be no ascensions to be made. Out of weakness he had spoken to the muscle.

And the muscle murmured wearily underneath the acres of swelling, and the black knew it would be cruel work there. Looking into the fire, he spoke questions to the femur and the fibula and the other bones he had known so well, that had been good to him in the past as the fine days were good to the hunter, as the old rocks had been good to the adolescent mountains, as the aged woods had been good to the proud new foliage when the earth came alive each springtime. And they too answered that they were frayed from the pain and the great weight of flesh they were bearing. Then in a sweating panic as the mighty wound hit him with agony again, Nebu cried out to the Lawgiver in his breast:

Heart, do I take the half-bwana to the white man's town? Do I have the strength to go all the way?

There were fearsome moments to listen to the deliberation of the Lawgiver, to the slow lunges of the hammer in his breast.

Is there a recompense to pay? the Lawgiver finally asked.

There is a recompense to pay.

And who will pay the recompense, Nebu? Are you the Wronged One?

I am to pay, he said unsteadily. I am to pay to the Wronged One.

Then why do you ask? Would you abandon the rules of your fathers?

And why not? shouted the weakness in him. *Can one half of man out-guile the white man's guns and fight the leopard and yet obey the rules?*

But the Lawgiver turned sadly away at his cowardice.

The pain darkened and Nebu keeled slowly over and thudded to the floor, six inches from the fire.

'Lord love a duck!' cried the boy excitedly as the African struggled up and sat again, his back to the wall, 'General Nebu you nearly croaked then!'

The negro said, an hour later, with his spear pointing up the distant swash to where instinct and a nose for the dwellings of the whites told him lay the road: 'Just beyond that hill is the white man's road. If I fall, you go on alone. You must go to the white man.'

The thin grey face whipped up to him. 'Alone? Are you crazy? With that leopard on our trail?'

Nebu saw the terror crease along his forehead and down the side of his face and run down into the thin bitter mouth.

'Would you stay and die with me?'

'D-die with you . . .?' Terror ran out of his mouth in a screaming torrent of words. 'You black fool! Give me the rifle. Give it to me, give it to me!'

He launched himself forward on the crutches. One birdlike hand clawed for the sling of the rifle on the black's shoulder. He tugged, screaming, at the sling.

'You Kikuyu ape! Filthy – filthy – filthy ape!'

Tears flowing obscenely down his face, he fought at the sling, waking the pain in Nebu's side. The negro stood immovable until one crutch slipped and the boy sprawled in the mud. He lay there

80

rieking and hammering his face in the mud. Nebu stood alone in
e land and held up his face to be washed by the friendly rain. He
ught water on his tongue and drank it greedily.

*

: had been with several bands before Koko's and had left them as
airs drove him. One had been led by M'lodi, a thick-set north
kuyu whom the British caught and hanged. The band had been
shed in retreat up the slopes to near the snow-line, far from
lages and game and women as the British lines deepened in men
d cannon and the planes wailed down from the skies and bombed
em. And those were the Days of Ache.
'We ache in our guts and below our guts from hunger,' M'lodi
e evening said, brutally as befits a leader. 'There is little game,
d no women. If we fire our guns it will bring the pink-cheeks on
. Be it known to all, then: we will eat shrubs and be wives to
rselves.'
And Nebu, although he had no cry for leadership beating in
m, had wondered why M'lodi, who every hour cried that he was
e leader, did not have the men cut bows and hunt game with
em. He spoke to one of the spearmen, and the spearman, who
ared M'lodi, told it to M'lodi to buy favour. So on this shivering
ld day M'lodi, in a terrible voice, called out Nebu before the band.
'Take off the white man's clothes!' bellowed M'lodi, jabbing the
l pea-jacket with his chief's stick.
Nebu looked around him at the hard set faces, and he knew the
ar thing it could be if he showed resistance. So he shed the jacket
d was a defenceless fellow before M'lodi in the wind. And M'lodi
nced with rage and shrieked:
'Now you are a native!' and whipped him on the naked shoulder
any times. 'Do you like being a native?' – a word pulled out with
s teeth. 'Do you want to be a naked bush native again?' Wealing
s back, washing his soul in pain and blood so that he would be
iter than snow.

And later, while he rubbed clay into the bloody weals, raw ː
fire, that M'lodi had given him, the lesson was fired in Nebu's mir
that the Days of Ache were also the Days of the Gun. He retrievᵉ
the spear and took off from the camp. M'lodi had whipped hi
because he had wanted to return to the Days of Wood, the Days ᵒ
the Bow. But after he went down the slope and saw here and the
through the trees the gaunt male limbs writhing on each other,
day's journey down where the m'pweki trees grew he cut a sine
from one of the m'pwekis and made himself a bow.

The unnatural M'lodi lost most of his troop and the Engliᵉ
caught him and slew him with a rope.

'The gun will not speak for you either,' Nebu, looking down, to
the back of the boy's head. 'The gun is for the bwanas.'

The boy flung himself around in the mud and the brown ey
blazed up at Nebu. 'Ignorant!' he screamed. 'Am I not a bwana?'

Nebu looked away, up the valley. He said thoughtfully: 'M
strength will not hold. And the leopard is impatient. Let us ⁱ
now.'

The rain fell quietly, austerely, silver threads leaking from a fin
punctured leaden bowl. Nebu thought of some journeys he hɑ
made before, the golden journeys, through sunlight and shinir
grass with coveys of francolins and spurfowl sporting on the hiⁱ
sides, and the orange-red redshanks wading in the blue lakes. Son
journeys had the severity of silver, those in the months of tˡ
'small rains', the cold December moon-days. There were journe
that were the dark journeys of midnight, with lighted fires in yoᵘ
side and the flames wrapping your loins and flowing down yoᵘ
thighs and legs and ankles – and a stalking leopard unafraid
your fires. Journeys that ran dark murmurs through your veins.

Nebu looked about him and he saw that already the teita we
out, blooming in fleecy white flowers that were born to scent tˡ
land only as long as the rains lasted. The rain-flowers. And tˡ
canarinas were comforting the sad, sodden trees, climbing all ᵘ
and around them and garlanding them with warm orange-tintᵉ
bells.

And looking about he saw these too:

The scarlet, upflung heads of the fireballs glowing defiance.

And the aromatic balsams, thick enough to hide buffaloes.

The many-fingered hands of forest ferns guarding the faces of the rocks; entombing those secrets hidden in the boles of dead trees.

And the blessed green hands of the murichis flinging cupfuls of fragrance and purple blooms all over the places he would walk.

Inside the earth, underneath his feet, inside the booming earth he felt the sliding and the settling of the humus fixing to shoot upward, to publish the tidings of a new creation. So in the soles of his feet Nebu prayed to his rude God.

Almighty God, he said to his rude God, *make my limbs mighty to withstand the journey and the leopard.*

He knew that stand of mwena over there. They flourished dark and tall and stout in their trunks and wore bright yellow spikes stuck fetchingly in their foliage. He knew the great grey baobab too. Under such a baobab had the tribe held market-place and council-place. And when they danced the ngoma all night until the sun rose, the whole company would shuffle and pound, moving sideways like an immense dark flower until they were beneath the baobab, in its shadow.

Baobab, Nebu spoke to the baobab tree as the pain struck him and reeled him to lean against the bole, *baobab, the white man's bullet is making me beautiful. Can one who stinks so be made beautiful?*

The baobab asked sternly: *What did the Lawgiver say to you?*

Nebu would not answer. He turned to the wound and asked gravely: *Wound, oh green garden growing in my side, is death to come when the flowers of poison open in me?* But the wound had its own rough ground to cover.

Nebu jabbed the point of his spear into the ground and came upright on it. He blinked, and saw the boy's eyes brightly intense on him. A motion of his hand signalled the boy on.

'Why don't you rest for a while?' the boy asked in a kind voice. 'The pain will go if you rest. Lie down and sleep, I will watch.'

The black grunted and motioned him on again. The boy stood his ground. Compassion was on his face.

'Moreover, Nebu,' he said soothingly, 'I do believe that the leopard has gone. For I tell you a strange thing: I cannot smell you any longer. It is healing, I am sure. Rest a while and help it along, eh, General Nebu?'

But Nebu touched the false boy with the point of his spear and indicated with his head again. And the brown doors swung open in the boy's eyes and Nebu saw the swift leap of anger before they closed again. The boy shook his head sadly.

'Then let me take your panga,' he pleaded. 'All these weapons are too heavy for you. You mustn't fall before we reach the road.'

The spear whirled in Nebu's hand and he slapped the boy with the flat of the butt.

'On, toto, on!' he commanded harshly.

The boy stumbled and recovered. He plodded forward, head and shoulders hunched against the rain. But he laughed silently and steadily as he went. The black had been talking to a tree! In the same unswerving way in which he listened when he swung on the horn of the moon, he was listening now for the African's fall. He had been neat, he knew; contained, implacable. The black would be fixed.

Nebu held out his hand for a butterfly to alight on it, clumsily flying with its weight of wet pollen. Half a mile downwind the leopard smelled the tainted wound, and began working upwind again.

21

The Land-Rover carried a light machine-gun, operated through a trap in the bullet-proof windscreen. There was also a Bren gun carrier, a World War Two model but as effective against the Kikuyu type of firepower as a knife on cheese. The army lieutenant had proof of it. He waved curtly to the men in the door of the police post and at the same time called out: 'Let's roll.'

The tiny convoy rolled out of the courtyard past the sentries at the gate and took the road.

The rain was pouring from a bottomless sky. The ropy rain tied the dark sky to the darker land, a liana-hung forest of water through which the vehicles seemed to hack a way. The Land-Rover's blunt prow lifted and waggled and shoved ahead, the carrier lurching after it. The land no longer rejoiced in the rain. It took its beating sullenly, gloomily, turning uneasily when the wind blew. The lieutenant with his gloved hand wiped the inner surface of the windscreen and thought of gentle Kentish rain and the smell of wet hops.

22

Nebu moved his feet carefully past each other, going slowly but with a proud bearing. He used the spear as a walking-stick; with his head conical in the cloak, he was a seven-foot prophet journeying between cities. The boy swung on a jerky rhythm before him. Except for the occasional clash of a water-soaked branch falling through a tree, they were alone in a wet silent world. The black had long ago concluded that the big trunk muscles would be the working muscles. If a man could sit and find a wall for his back, he could fight off a leopard. He knew he was on stilts from the flexors of his hip-joint downwards: down there, there was neither anger, nor love, nor even weariness. It puzzled him that there was no Nebu down there, yet, when he looked down, there were the legs moving past each other, pompous as turkeys. He laughed at them, a huge joke bottled inside his head. But the big trunk muscles were different. They still held strength.

He wrote a poem to the big trunk muscles and sang it as he went pompously on.

'O mighty sinews, given me by my father and my mother,

'O massive towers that encompass the hills of my shoulders and the plateau of my neck, the valley of my belly,

'O cry of power rising in me like the songs of a thousand warriors,

'Give me the flight of the hawk, to soar for ever, because my strength will not permit me to bound to earth!

'Give to me the roar of the lion, whose bravery will not consent for him to be quiet;

86

'Give to me the fortitude of the camel, to grunt only and not to weep when I am ill-used;

'Give to me the authority of the sun, so that none will look me in the eye;

'Give to me the dominion of the moon, that all ugly things lose their ugliness when I look at them.'

He worked his shoulders under the rubber sheet and shrugged off the pools of water. He touched the boy, guiding him away from the trees. He knew that when the leopard struck again it would strike with even more ferocity than guile, so he kept away from the trees. It had been foiled before and the black knew that somewhere among those trees it was pacing them, now running downwind, now gliding swiftly in the other direction, tail twitching and eye unwinking, pausing to wash its face and to yawn, standing so still sometimes it could have been a painted rock.

Nebu unslung the rifle and carried it at the trail. The day before yesterday it had hampered him. He had noticed the unbalance at his back when he had fought off the leopard with his spear. Today was a weaker day. No day for a handicap. He carried the rifle along in his left hand and tried not to think how fitting the weapon felt in his hand. He looked down at it, brought it up nearer to his eyes, and it was all there, just as Koko's had been, and not alien at all. His wrong must have been monstrous for him to have been inflicted with the great wound, a false boy and a rifle that would not speak. He looked at it and shook it gently.

'No use praying to it,' the boy's pert voice broke in on him. 'It will *not* shoot for you.'

He looked like the figures which the white men placed in their fields to scare away the crows, Nebu thought wearily: the shoulders that jumped up into little peaks each time the crutches hit the ground, the pitiably thin body as it swung between the uprights of his sad little house.

'Why will it not speak for me?' Nebu asked curtly. 'Am I worse than the others?'

'Much worse. You will not trust the white man.'

'Trust – trust which white man?' Nebu asked, flabbergasted.

'Me,' the boy replied aggrievedly. 'You have never trusted me since we met. Have you not been taught to trust the bwanas?'

The mask of head and face nodded in the white man's manner. 'To obey him as he obeys his God, who tells him to turn the other cheek, not to repay evil for evil. Nebu has been wounded in his side by a piece of bread.'

'You only got what you deserved. You should have stayed away from our camp.'

'How could I obey if I stayed away?'

Sometimes it was better to joke than to write poetry. He could listen for the answers. Poetry fetched no answer. You wrote it in your head and sang it, just as trees grew and the blossoms fell. There was no answer to falling leaves; unless you called the new trees that sprung where the leaves fell the answers. And it was no answer; it was something new. Unless you thought of it as a cycle, without beginning or ending. The sap rose in spring, the trees flourished in summer, leaves fell in autumn and the whole died when the snows flew. But again the sap rose in spring. Poetry could be like the falling leaves if there was a son to sing the verses you made, after you had died. The African looked at the crooked question-sign flailing along before him and he asked:

'There are many magic things done by the white man's doctors; could they not have strengthened the young bwana's foot?'

The boy stopped abruptly. Then his back hunched and his head went down and he stood miserably in the rain. A thin line of wonder slipped into Nebu's head. He slung the rifle to his shoulder and reached out a hand to touch the boy. But he withdrew it quickly; and suddenly, uncannily, he was singing, a sliver of sound in his throat. The boy turned the dead face up to him.

'My father gave me a crooked foot, something special to mark me from the rabble. Do you object, black?' he asked fiercely.

The African felt the mud rising up past his face, drowning him. He looked numbly past the boy. A sort of grin crinkled the grey face.

'Don't you agree I look – different?' whispered the grey boy. 'Where is your tongue? Flown away? Answer me, Kike! You ashamed of what my father gave me?'

He looked at the boy. His eyes fell. 'The – the young bwana mocks me,' Nebu said humbly. 'He makes a joke at me.'

The old-young face considered it. 'Mock you? Joke at you? Yes, I suppose so. Only stop asking me foolish questions and we will get along famously. You see, Kikuyu?'

'Yes, young bwana,' Nebu said, head down.

The boy regarded him closely. Suddenly he said: 'Now I am a little weary. I think you should carry me. Bend down so I may climb to your shoulder.'

It was two months' journey to the ground, an immeasurable space between his knees and the ground, a year of merciless days, a time of reluctant bones and flesh, and pain that giggled and shrieked in him. He murdered himself going to his knees. He floated up with the boy sitting on his shoulders. The crown of his head flew off and went whirling over the far hill.

'Go slowly, so it won't hurt much,' the boy said kindly to the weaving negro. 'March gently, Nebu, so it won't kill you.'

Suffer, the black said. *Suffer, so it won't hurt much.*

The boy giggled and suppressed it and said rapidly: 'It is very nice up here, very nice indeed when you are high up. Look, Nebu! Do you know there are darters more than twenty inches across the wings? When they are over the water, they fly fast and impale the fish on their beaks when they dive, then throw them up in the air and catch them again coming down. Gulp, they swallow him. Poor fish.'

Few bwanas know that, Nebu cried proudly. *Nor do they know of the sandpipers who are brown out of season, but turn mottled chestnut when they breed. Nor that the female of the spurfowl also wears a spur. You can flush them by barking like a dog.*

'I can see the fireballs, red as blood and marching with us!' the boy cried excitedly. 'And the gloriosi are sucking the tall mutomas to death through their leaves!'

Few of the white men know that the monsonia shuts in the afternoon, Nebu sang triumphantly in reply. *Nor that the mwethia, the canary-bush, grows ten feet tall and dies with the new moon. The toto is learned.*

The boy laughed high-pitched and happy. 'Nebu! General Nebu, you are the general's horse! You hold your head high as the general's horse!'

High as the general's horse, Nebu cried happily, ignoring the terrible uprootings in his side caused by the boy's jabbing heel.

He strode gravely, stiffly, along, walking the spear beside him. This was how he would have re-entered Koko's camp, head up and spear up, or – no, the rifle princely borne.

'Procession!' the boy cried far above his head.

It is the warriors coming in for a big ngoma, Nebu echoed. *A dance of praise for a fine boy.*

'Procession!' the heels kicking into his sick body. 'Procession! The leopard has come out to join us!'

And where are the lordly lions? the African asked inside of him. *And the fleet gazelles? The elephants? We should see the lions going home from their kills, blood-flecked and filled. And the old hippo, grunting and rushing at his shadow. Tell me when the great pythons curve from the bush, from among the sweet-scented balsam. Tell me what you see of my land, toto. I would go blindly.*

The leopard bounded grandly from the balsam over a hundred yards behind them and focused his yellow-green eyes on the two humans ahead. Behind the hard-boned forehead there was just a faint wonder at the fantasia of two sure kills who walked before him and were not afraid. He padded on calmly, only slightly put out that already one of them smelled so highly of putrefaction.

'You carry me just as my father used to do,' the boy said softly to the damp curly hair, two fistfuls of which he clutched. 'You are good for a black.'

Procession! Nebu cried to the agony inside. *To the ngoma!*

23

The leopard was a great dog at the mouth of the cave. Nebu and the boy were safe in there. The leopard loved them and would watch over them that no danger entered the cave. Now and again the triangular head went down, sniffing unmistakably of the scents Nebu had left there when he had dragged himself across the threshold. The rain fell heavily on the sodden coat and twinkled in frozen drops on the nap of the jaws. It stretched its hind-legs one after the other, shaking off the water, and doubled the thick neck to lick the water from its underside. Nebu, his back to the concave wall, thought on the strangeness of a cat sitting in the rain.

He had fallen three times, or maybe four, but the boy had been very good about it, standing and waiting patiently until he had struggled again to his knees, before he climbed to his shoulders. He had been a good rider, only applying the spur when Nebu stumbled. Most bwanas would not have been so considerate. He had long ago thrown away the crutches.

After Nebu had dragged himself to the end of the cave, he had sat down with the massively swollen legs stretched out before him, legs belonging in another country. They were beautiful things, greenish in places, large as trees, all the hollows rounded out so that he had to guess where the ankles must have turned and the tendons used to make their quick labours. He bent at his waist and with his hands lifted one of the legs and wondered who was the stranger.

'The young bwana could borrow these for his journey to the road,' he said.

The boy was wedged into an overhang of the wall. Outwardly

91

stiff as ice, inside he literally churned with fury at the black for entering the cave. He had tried to keep him going towards the road, but the ignorant Kikuyu had spied the cave and lumbered for it, unturnable as a mountain. He had tried kicking him viciously in the side; the black seemed to have lost the sense of feel after the first fall. He looked in disgust at the barrel-shaped body. The swollen nigger stank. He looked back at the painted cat and was instantly frozen with terror again. There was something he should do but he could not rightly remember what that was. It was funny, the way the terror held him: he could think, but not move. He was an effigy, he thought brightly, fixed forever in grey stones.

The weapons were laid out beside Nebu, the spear, the panga and the rifle. Nebu breathed regularly and felt quite healthy. The cave went in deep, bulging at one side into a good-sized room. A couple of large rocks that had evidently fallen from the roof a long time ago, tall as a man, had rolled into the bulge. He thought they would make an effective barrier for the door, but he was too comfortable to move. Moreover, the leopard had come calling and it was not tribal custom to spurn the visitor. He called softly:

'Brother Leopard, come in out of the wet.'

But he had spoken too early. Custom demanded that there be a longer wait before you spoke. Brother Leopard was a better African then he. Nebu lowered his head and looked hurtfully at the leopard. A good cat too, lean-flanked and quiet. He'd bet the coat was unmarred. That tail would be splendid to flick with in the largest council meeting. It would be worthy for a king. A token beast, well worth his hide. The women would have clapped their hands in the slow beats of applause when you portered him into the village. The sub-chiefs would have gathered about you and nodded the slow nods of approval. And perhaps the chief himself would have strode out of his hut looking neither to the right nor the left but long and keenly at the dead brute and touched your shoulder with his fan of ostrich feathers. But such things were gone.

The villages had gone, the chiefs were servants in Nairobi factories and the women whored in Government Road. Left were just these: a leopard waiting at the door, and a boy cowering his false face into his armpit, and poison warping your sick body. He spat into the dust of the cave.

Sing, blood! Nebu sang defiantly. *Sing of the strength seated in the back and the shoulders and the arms. Sing to Brother Leopard to come, leaping in for his meal like the noble animals.*

The boy shuddered and looked up out of the refuge of his armpit. 'You said you would have taken me to the road. You have failed the young bwana,' he accused.

'The white man's road is like the sands of Kilindini, unending,' Nebu said garrulously. 'Like the sea at Kilindini, immovable. You will go to the white man's road. You will cross it sometime, somewhere.'

'When I am dead,' the boy said woodenly.

'No,' the African said, his face glistening in the half-light of the cave. 'No, the young bwana will never die. He will live forever like the white man's road.'

'My father taught me your tongue,' the boy said out of nothing, and his body moved, unflexing arms and legs, shooting emotion into his face. 'My father said I would never know when it would come in useful. He said most of the whites, being fools, never learnt the Kikuyu tongue. He was a fool, but he was useful.'

'Why do you say he was a fool?'

The boy rested the crippled foot across his forearm and leaned towards Nebu, his eyes shining. 'You reminded me of him today, when you allowed me to ride you. All the way through the forest, after I had thrown away the crutches, he made me ride him.'

'You – threw away the crutches?'

The grey face lost the light. He said sullenly: 'Lost them. Why do you ask silly questions?'

A good laugh is like a free march, Nebu thought, *all your limbs joyous, hearing no sob in the cry of the curlew, brushing through the nettles grasping at your feet as if they were a field of daisies.* The forced laughter in his head was like a forced march; the dust of it rose up to choke him.

'The young bwana lived in Nairobi?'

'Out in Parklands,' the boy said, alive again. 'A big house with many servants, and I had a stout Somali woman to lift me up and down stairs. We got along famously. She never reported me to my father but she often cried. Her face was not cut from lumber, as was the dog's, and yours.'

'The dog's? Lumber? Mine?' Nebu asked confusedly.

The boy was furious. 'Who said that?' he shouted. 'You are an ignorant black!'

The leopard stirred at the shout and the eyes burned steadily in on them. Nebu's hand silently sought the shaft of the spear. The boy froze in the overhang of the wall, his eyes blank with terror.

'Enter, Brother Leopard,' Nebu said softly. 'Let us begin our talk now.'

The pain hit dully, growling deep and strong as an organ. The toto had lied. He was false all through.

24

'Tell me about your mother,' Nebu said after a time of twisting and sweating and gasping. He was struggling up out of the bowels of the earth, calling to the first glimmer of light, identifying himself again with being alive.

But the boy's skin and bones were bondservants to the presence of the leopard. He sat still as the print in a book.

I will tell you, went the voice in Nebu's head. *Her eyes were the sunflowers in April, blue as the lipwe flower. Her breasts were snow-covered peaks. I will tell you: on Mount Kenya is virgin snow and only the sunlight may lay weight on it. Her limbs were long and cool as the river. You hide behind the bushes and bathe in the pools, but it is forbidden to bathe in the open. She was a woman who lived beyond my ridge, a thought of last year's thunder, a whisper of a drum in the night, a bird that flew up from a far bush, a long-forgotten garden in which you planted your young trees.*

He leaned forward, his great shoulders swaying, and the choir sang grandly in his head: *I will tell you. She was the forbidden road on which Nebu walked. It led to the hut of the king. But should a warrior be afraid of his king?*

Then his voice opened, booming inside the cave, rolling off the fluted roof: 'A man should not love unless he seeks death. Love is death, Nebu. You die in the one you love. A little love is a little death, the big love is the big death. Nebu died the big death when he returned to the herd and heard the drum beaten with the back of the hand.'

But his loins laughed.

'Loins . . .?' he said angrily, and stopped.

He fell silent and looked at the animal in the doorway. It had not moved. It was growling in the uneasy halls of its belly. Cowering behind the growl was the mad scream leopards sometimes make. His long ebony fingers trembled on the spear.

'Which of them, then, did Nebu love big?' he shot at the boy. 'Her, or the msabu?'

But the grey boy was in a grey death, his limbs knotted and still.

'Loins,' Nebu demanded, 'speak, then. Which did you love most? The girl or the msabu?'

But I was blind! his loins protested. My eyes were closed when I sang.

'But was there any difference in your singing?' Nebu persisted. 'Was your singing more splendid for the black woman or for the white woman?'

Is today's rain different from yesterday? retorted his loins. Does it rain lead today and gold yesterday? Will the moon at next harvest be larger or smaller than the last?

'Ha, ha, ha,' Nebu laughed, floating along on waves of agony. 'I may not be here to tell you.'

Then leave the question with your nearest kinsman.

The smell of what he had, enriched the cave. If he had been home, it would have enriched his home ridge and the next and the one after that, all the land of the Kikuyus. The Council of Nine would have removed him to a far place in the bush and left him with his spear. But the Council of the Two, the Bwana and his Bullet, had done the same thing for him. *A man is never, while he is on the earth, far from his home,* thought Nebu. *But there is no home in these lawless days.*

*

There are three ridges in the land of the Kikuyu: Nyeri, Kiambu and Muranga. Mine was the ridge of Nyeri, in the village of Kitusi, where the cook-fires were never out. It was the law. We herded the

96

oats in the day and learnt to set traps for the coney and lesser
udu, for the smaller antelope and the bush pig, and in the evening
e sat at the feet of the elders and learnt the steps for the ngoma
nd words of the old songs. This was the law. And we obeyed and
rew and were taught the spear and bow and panga and not to lie.
his was the law.

We did not stray from the law of our territory, nor from the rule
f our chosen men in the Council of Nine. Where a man obeys the
w, there is his home. The lawless man is homeless.

*

Ha, ha, ha. Loins, are you still alive? Have you got a home?'
  But his loins muttered vexedly.
  'Bones,' Nebu asked worriedly, 'are you still alive?'
  Some, the lower ones, were bound with dead muscles, but the
hers answered bravely.
  'Trunk, are you powerful? Will you be mighty when I want
ou?'
  He braced his shoulders so that the blades met. His chest bulged
ke the corner-keep of a castle. The leopard twisted its head to one
de and bawled into the cave.

25

They had left the vehicles a mile or two behind and had penetrate
the valley on a short foot patrol. The lieutenant halted at the roa
of the leopard.

He asked: 'What was that?'

The guide, a crusty, fed-up-with-walking old Kenya hand
grunted: 'Only a leopard. Probably made a kill.'

The lieutenant, younger by a score of years, poorer by thousand
of pounds, but God's vicar when on a patrol, said: 'Let's go an
hunt him down.'

'What for?' demanded the guide angrily as the excellent coffee
planting rain ran off his helmet. 'Are we hunting Kikes or leopards?

'Good stalking practice for my men,' vouchsafed the lieutenant.

'But at this rate we will be out for a week!'

'It came from over there,' the lieutenant said, moving forwar
His patrol went in single file behind him. He grinned his hard gri
and thought of the sad things: a lost dog, an odd shoe, a pot-bellie
coffee-planter aching to return to his plantation.

The ground was soggy, but sharp-pointed stones stuck up lik
thorns out of the mud. He walked carefully, thinking God kne
what He was doing when He placed pads on the feet of the cats. H
wondered how the blacks managed to walk barefooted around her
They had no pads, nor boots. God must have hated these blacks
have dumped them in places like these. He himself didn't min
them if they behaved themselves and kept out of his way. Th
thought made him feel magnanimous, kindlier than God. His bi
body, under the loosely hung leather windbreaker, drove ahead.

26

The leopard made soft noises in its throat and its head sank a little between the forepaws. Behind, its legs scrabbled softly on the floor. The tremors ran from its stiffening tail along the spine to the neck. The neck was filling up, hooding.

'Toto, don't move,' Nebu warned.

The warm rich blood was pumping forth along the African's veins, approving in a murmur the wakefulness of his biceps, saluting the great leaps of his pectorals when he breathed in. He felt the strength coil into his forearms and replace his fingers with steel springs. He was being acclaimed from all sides. Suddenly, the boy was unknotted. He looked at the black and looked at the leopard fixing its limbs in the door of the cave.

'He is coming in now,' he said, far off as the South Pole. 'He is coming in to eat us.'

'He is coming in to die,' Nebu said.

'You will miss. You are weak. I kicked you in the wound. You cannot throw.'

'I can throw even when I am dead,' Nebu boasted. 'I can split him between his eyes, in mid-air.'

He could split an elephant, with the potency he felt prowling through his body. He could tie the River Tana into a knot; hoist Fort Hall past his eyebrow.

'I will split him so that both halves will climb straight up my spear.'

'You are a fool,' the boy said, weary and sick down there in the cold. He held something out to Nebu. 'Here – fix this to the rifle and it will shoot.'

Nebu looked quickly down and then swung his eyes back to the cat. The toto was not only false, but a fool too. It was a poor payment he was handing to Bwana Gibson's people. But there was no other coin. He had no goats nor sheep nor cattle nor beloved wife.

'It is the bolt of the rifle. It must have been wrenched out when my father fell,' the boy said without artifice.

Nebu risked another quick look. But his head sang: *False! The toto is false as a worm's skull!* The toto had been endeavouring to murder him back there on the trail even while he spoke the honeyed words. And even now, in the presence of the leopard which was making up its mind to kill, he was being false. Was there no limit to the boy's hate? Gently, not to disturb the fine balance in his body, Nebu shook his head.

'Nebu,' the boy said softly. The black looked curiously at him.

'You love me very much,' the boy said.

The boy's eyes were opened wide, stretched boldly wide so that they were two huge, strangely lit rooms into which the black almost wandered. Nebu was glad that the great bow on his back snubbed on the threshold and halted him. His legs were sleek and firm once more and he backed away proudly on them. The Negro laughed in his belly; it was unseen on his face.

'I love you, toto?'

The boy said quickly: 'I have thought it out. I know why you love me very much.'

'The young bwana speaks in riddles,' Nebu said gravely.

The ground was deep and springy underneath his feet, as it used to be. Through the soles of his feet he was sounding his continent and he could hear the wheatfields in the uplands rejoicing that Nebu the Farmer was back.

'Bwana, fiddlesticks,' the boy grinned. 'I know why. You are my father.'

Nebu had grown out of the cave. He was three days' journey out

f his sickness. The wanderobo twanged and the seven-foot spear
ing, and game ran wailing through the bush that Nebu the
Hunter was back.

'Father,' the boy said softly, grinning at him.

Through the soles of his feet, he could hear the ocean at Mom-
asa. The great waves stood straight up in the water, fifty yards
ut, and tossed their shaggy heads and roared in and shook the
each in their teeth.

The negro said gently: 'Then you know, toto. I would not have
urt the half-bwana by telling him. For then you could not return
o Parklands to the big house and play with the children of the
hite men.'

The eyes of the boy closed tightly on the pain. 'My mother was
hite,' he said slowly.

'She – she was the woman of a warrior!' Nebu cried.

The boy's eyes opened. The pain was gone and they were clear.

'My father is a warrior,' he said, his head up. 'Nebu, the warrior.
love him very much.'

Heart! whispered Nebu fearfully to the mighty leap within him.
Would you die at the good news?

'A great warrior,' Nebu said gravely. 'Alone, Nebu slew a bwana
ho carried a rifle. It is a greater feat than to kill an elephant.'

'You will kill the leopard too,' the boy said quickly. 'I know you
ill.'

'Easily,' Nebu said.

'Especially if you use the rifle. Take the bolt. I will show you how
is to be fitted.'

'No, toto,' Nebu said gently. 'I know the spear. A great warrior is
nsible. He does not ride a strange horse over a narrow footbridge.'

The boy shuddered. His bitter mouth opened widely at the black.

'Fool! Filthy Kikuyu!' he shrieked. 'I hid the bolt from you! Take
and shoot the leopard – now!'

Nebu bowed his head as the blow reached him. He was back in
e cave. He saw his obese thighs waxing in poison and smelled the
is. He raised his tortured face to the boy.

'No,' Nebu whispered humbly. 'Not again, half-bwana!'

'Stupid – idiot – then shoot him!' shrieked the boy.

The shiny bolt shot from the boy's hand to the racked, swollen lap of the black. The boy flung himself across Nebu's knees fighting to get at the rifle which lay on the far side of the Negro Roused and angered, Nebu picked up the bolt and threw it from him.

'No!' he roared. 'No – you are false! False! he stormed. Then th cat must have given a warning to the African, for in a swift chang of mood, he said under his breath: 'Be still!'

A sudden, almost unseen change had descended on the anima Clearly, to Nebu, the leopard had made up his mind to charge.

But he will come in low, Nebu worried. *And it is much too dar in the cave to be throwing close to the ground. Come in high, M Leopard, so that I may have you high above the ground. Then ther will be your large heart to split.*

'But no matter, Brother Leopard,' Nebu said as he aimed th spear. 'I think you will come as I want you. It is ordained.'

And there he stuck, aiming like a fool, while the world double up in laughter at him. For, with a cry curling back from him, th boy had hurled himself after the bolt as it twisted in the ai And the long supple god, made of leopard, left the floor in a grea leap.

'Toto!' Nebu cried from his belly, 'flatten down, toto!'

For the leopard had come in high and he was good to get in th air. But the boy wanted the bolt, the little piece of luck he ha saved to himself when, through struggle after struggle with hin self on the trail, fear had nearly defeated his resolution to be rid the taunt which, on that unforgettable day at the commencemer of the safari. Gibson had pinned on his back. With mad cunnin; the planter had caught a glimpse of what lay behind the brow doors in the boy's eyes. He had allowed him no chances.

*

102

'Toto!' Explosively. Tearingly.

But halt the tides at Kilindini, as halt the boy.

And the yellow eyes in the wicked head fastened larger and larger on the boy.

The cat-bellow tearing from his throat, the leopard went up on his arc, forepaws up and hindlegs down, power and glory in the arrogant slant of the head, the exposed fangs, the three-inch claws unsheathing. And the final, shattering roar felled the roof on Nebu as the cat swept down on its mark.

The flying beast settled and Nebu's ear caught the quick crunch. The black lowered his head and peered at the boy and the slayer from under his brows. He was weeping. He blinked and muttered.

'Slow toto,' Nebu muttered. 'Poor slow toto. You should have told me of the bolt long ago, then you would not now be in Brother Leopard's arms.'

He broke into loud laughter, and knew how strange it was that he should at the same time be weeping, and could stop doing neither. He leaned forward, shaking the spear.

'To me, Brother Leopard!' he cried at the reptilian head. 'Here is better recompense – take me!'

The leopard growled. The boy was still. Outside the cave, the land creaked and groaned under the weight of the water. Nebu spoke to his muscles as he wept. He kept jabbing the spear at the beast.

27

Nebu was laughing his head off. The aloe trees in his throat shed bitter blooms of mirth up and down and across in him. The angry laughter rioted in his belly and in the rooms behind the bones of his forehead, and dug at the hinges of his jaws so badly that he thought he screamed with pain. But the scream came out of him as a wild noise of hilarity. He could not understand it at all. He would surely explode, so hard did he try to hold it in. And he was cold; freezingly cold. He wanted to be warm but he was already dead. The worms had got to him. The arm out there moving the spear so that it tongued impudently at the leopard, holding him at bay, did not belong to him.

Whose arm are you? his eyes asked the arm.

The arm of Bwana Gibson, said the insolent arm.

The maddened cat raged in another country. He looked unconcernedly at the cat: a cat being furious on a far ridge unconnected with his country. He felt roughed by the cold. Sleep would smooth him warmly out. But the choleric cat was entertaining, the way it fought and bit the air.

'Where are you from, Brother Leopard?' he called across the ridge. 'Where do you rule, King Leopard? Did you cross the lands of the Kikuyus to dance before Bwana Arm?'

No. He shook his head emphatically as he laughed. *No, no, no.*

Not the lands of my people. The Chuka, the Mbere, the Mwimbi, the Embu, the Meru, the Kichugu, the Tharaka, the Ndia, the Muthamba, all the race of Kikuyu. Not across the lands of the Kikuyus.

We drew back into our forests, King Leopard, and dug our war-pits and none could follow. We were invincible to black and white warriors. None would follow and we never came out. We were the Shy Children who stung when we were followed.

We burnt the papyrus to obtain our salt, and drank the blood of our cattle from the jugular. Our women fed on the milk of goats and bore children more numerous than the nuggets mined by the Great One in the evening sky. His voice came stoutly out again:

'You are strong as the oak tree,' he said admiringly to the arm. It had a fine blue trunk and this wood would live for a thousand years. The leopard would be broken on it.

We were the Shy Children of the forests, King Leopard, against whom the guns of the white warriors failed. But their gifts prevailed.

And he was suddenly clear-headed at that, and he thought: *A man's pride is mostly broken by gifts.* Peering at the leopard as it raged beyond the perimeter of the spear, he thought the pride of the leopard had been in his patience, the cat quality of waiting: to go thoroughly away into silence and only become alive when it was time to kill. Patience was one kind of pride.

He said softly: 'Your pride, your patience, was destroyed by the gift of the toto. You could not resist the gift of himself which he offered you. Yet your patience would have given both of us to you.

'Now will you eat neither of us!' he bellowed, lunging with the spear.

The cat hurled itself backward in a frightful uproar. It alighted and whirled fast, all around on itself like a top, furiously slashing its claws at nothing.

Nebu, ignoring it, looked down at the boy. He knew his land, its trees and the savage life it spawned; and he knew that the leopard would not attack while he thought his victim strong and ready. So he looked down at the broken recompense on the floor, the twisted little cripple. A single downstroke of a paw had done it. He had died quickly, quietly.

'What was *your* pride, half-bwana?' Nebu queried softly. The bad laughter had left him. 'To hinder as the crooked thorn-bush hinders the foot of the traveller? Then you lost your pride, toto. You lost your pride and, instead of hindering, you tried at the last to help – even if you tried to help yourself. So you lost, toto, you lost.'

And it was as if he had written out an epitaph. He turned his head away, the mask-face incurious.

It was fine that he was almost without pain now. Only the purpling shapelessness down there and the smell. He felt lazily good, sleepy as in the late evening, as if evening, the long shadows, were lengthening in him. His head rested on Kinangop and his feet in the Ulu hills where the Kamba people dwelled. He laughed, sleepily, the length of his poisoned, dying world.

'But what is the bwanas' pride?' he questioned sharply, his head on one side, listening. But nobody answered him. 'Then I will ask in their cities. Property? That is all men's pride. Women? That pride also belongs to all men. To win? All men desire to win.'

But only a few may win, went his head. *Yet each one who loses helps another to win. So the man who loses may be prideful that he has won.* The bwanas boasted of it. Even while they were being made beautiful by fire or the knife, they boasted of the others who would come after them.

Then – then perhaps the bwanas' pride may be their strength in losing?

It rapped smartly again for notice.

The strength to lose an age and gain a generation, to lose customs, women, land, life to the wring of change. And you could pocket a sunbeam easier than lure the march of change into a war-pit. You could not defeat it. Each year, in the spring, change marched across his country, from Mombasa to the big mountains, and new flowers opened and new foals kicked wounds into the tender land. Change was invincible.

He said sadly: 'M'lodi, the unnatural, was right. I should have been strong and lost the bow, for the days of the bow have gone.'

And when he felt the pain rolling back into him, he said to it

'Perhaps I lie here, hurt and alone, because I had not the strength to lose the old customs but must go to Nairobi to pay the recompense.' The pain bounced inside his skull and he gasped and said: 'It is a braver deed to accept change than to enter the country of an enemy.'

And then the jewelled eyes tipped right over in his dim face and he sagged a little.

Nebu! Nebu! he thought he heard the leopard scream and he jerked up his head. The beast was back on its haunches, tail straight out and quivering at the tip. The yellow eyes, half closed, had completed the calculations. Nebu looked lazily at the cat. Funny, what was happening in the cat did nothing to him: the shock ripples at its shoulders, the flattened, hungry haunches, the tiny quick movements of the hind-legs searching for the take-off. He only knew that the evening, the long brown shadow off the Aberdares, had entered into him and was disposing itself in much of him.

'Oho, Brother Leopard, evening is in my belly but bright morning is in my arm,' he said softly. And the formidable spear rose easily to his shoulder and power flowed along his arm.

'I can throw,' Nebu boasted, 'from the Plains of Athi to the highlands. With evening sitting in my belly, even then I can throw.'

'Thank you, arm,' he told it gravely. 'I will dance at your ngoma, arm.'

When his eyes open wide, he will come, sang the black.

When his tail stiffens and the ripples die along his back, he will come.

When the hood at his neck fills out as mine filled out when I sang my first male-song into the heat and velvet of my first woman in the love-hut of Kikuyu, then he will come.

Instantly.

And he will die unquenched as my first love died.

Ready, Bwana Leopard, ready!

But the leopard did not come. For the army lieutenant fired into the cave.

28

The Englishman fired again into the body of the leopard and he was sure it was quite dead.

'Now let's have a look at what the bastard had cornered there.'

He waved the men away from the entrance so that he had some light as he entered. He saw the huddle of the boy and he stepped round the cat. He turned over the body.

'By God!' he rattled, 'It looks like a white boy . . . shoes on . . .'

He stooped and turned the face up, his brutal hands strangely tender. It came easily round on the broken neck.

'Like a bloody muddy flower on a bloody broken stem,' he brooded, helplessly savage. 'Wonder whose kid he was.'

He looked around the cave. His eyes picked up the black at the end and he streaked to his feet, gun pointing. But there was no movement there.

'Robbed me of my first Kike too, eh, Brother Leopard?'

He raised the gun and considered firing into the black just to make sure, then he recalled that they both seemed to have been travelling together. This must have been one of the loyal bucks, perhaps saved the child from a massacre. He dropped his arm and walked forward. He stood out hard against the light from the door, a lean-waisted, wide-shouldered, tawny bull leopard. And Nebu charted the curvature of his chest through the khaki bush jacket and marked where the breast-bone swelled above the heart, and the certainty that he had the target well laid flowed sweetly through him.

Great One, the African sang in his head, *give us long knives*.

It was morning in his arms and shoulders.

Further Reading

Background

Donald L. Barnett and Karari Njama, *Mau Mau from Within* (Monthly Review Press, New York & London, 1966).

Edward Kamau Brathwaite, 'The African Presence in Caribbean Literature', *Daedalus*, Spring 1974, pp. 73–109. Also in *Slavery, Colonialism and Racism* ed. Sidney W. Mintz (Norton, New York, 1974) pp. 73–109.

G. R. Coulthard, *Race and Colour in Caribbean Literature* (Oxford University Press, London, 1962).

O. R. Dathorne, 'Africa in the Literature of the West Indies', *The Journal of Commonwealth Literature*, No. 1, September 1965, pp. 95–116.

Jomo Kenyatta, *Facing Mount Kenya* (Vintage Books, New York, 1965; Heinemann, London, 1979). First published in 1938.

James Ngugi, *Weep Not, Child* (Heinemann, London, 1964).

— *A Grain of Wheat* (Heinemann, London, 1967).

Ngugi wa Thiong'o, 'Mau Mau, Violence and Culture', *Homecoming* (Heinemann, London, 1972) pp. 26–30. A book review first published in 1963.

V. S. Reid, *New Day* (Heinemann, London, 1973). First published in 1949.

— *The Jamaicans* (Institute of Jamaica, revised edition 1978). First published in 1976.

Carl G. Rosberg, Jr., and John Nottingham, *The Myth of 'Mau Mau': Nationalism in Kenya* (Praeger, New York & London, 1966).

Criticism

W. I. Carr, 'Vic Reid's Treatment of Race and Politics', *The Sunday Gleaner* (Kingston, Jamaica) 9 July, 1961.

O. R. Dathorne, 'Africa in the Literature of the West Indies', *The Journal of Commonwealth Literature*, No. 1, September 1965, pp. 112–13.

Barrie Davies, 'Neglected West Indian Writers, No. 2', *World Literature Written in English*, Vol. 11, No. 2, November 1972, pp. 83–5.

Louis James, 'Of Redcoats and Leopards', *The Islands in Between*, ed. Louis James (Oxford University Press, London, 1968), pp. 64–72.

Mark Kinkead-Weekes, ' "Africa" – Two Caribbean Fictions', *20th Century Studies*, No. 10, 1973, pp. 37–59.

Kenneth Ramchand, *The West Indian Novel and its Background* (Faber and Faber, London, 1970), pp. 154–9.

Gregory Rigsby, Introduction to V. S. Reid, *The Leopard* (Collier Books, New York, 1971), pp. 7–17.